The Day The Drum Stopped

and Other Stories

The Day
The Drum
Stopped

and Other Stories

Robert Loesch

Love and peace)
Robert Loesch

The cited quotation in "Six Candles" is from *Stories and Prose Poems* by Alexander Solzhenitsyn, published by Farrar, Straus and Giroux, New York, 1971; translation in English; copyright by Mike Glenny. The title of the excerpt is "The City on the Neva."

Book design by The Troy Bookmakers

Printed in the United States of America

The Troy Book Makers • Troy, New York • thetroybookmakers.com

To order additional copies of this title, contact your favorite local bookstore or visit www.tbmbooks.com

ISBN: 978-1-61468-119-9

For my children Shelley, Donald, Christine, and Sandra,
my son-in-law Francois, and my daughter-in-law Kathy,
for their reading pleasure.

Contents

Preface

I wrote this collection of ten short stories to entertain and inform my readers. The sequence of the stories is chronological. They draw upon my interests in people, history, culture, and travel. All the stories come from my imagination but are based upon some of my travels and work experiences.

"The Day the Drum Stopped" and "George Hendee – Bicycle Champion" are based on communities where I lived and worked: Madison, Connecticut; and Springfield, Massachusetts. "Natasha's Epiphany Gift" and "Six Candles" emerged from places I visited in Russia before the collapse of the Soviet Union. "Too Many Voices" and "No Blue Cheese, Please," which are based in Troy, New York, reflect my work with adults with mental illness and developmental disabilities. "My Sister, the Nurse" and "The Old Man" developed from my travels in Puerto Rico. The ninth story, "First Night" is also based in Springfield. The final story, "The Washington Park Snowman Contest" is set in Troy, New York.

Each of these stories depicts characters who deal with important daily situations and problems that are representative of many people. I have enjoyed creating and writing these stories. I hope that these stories entertain and help you, the reader, navigate through your own daily life in positive ways.

The Day the Drum Stopped

East Guilford, Connecticut, 1801

The day the drum stopped was a sad day for Ezekiel Hutchins. On that day in 1801 the Congregational Church of East Guilford replaced its church drum with a new bell in the tower. The bell would call people throughout the Connecticut village to meetings and worship.

Ezekiel Hutchins, fifty-five years old, had lived with his mother and father, Hannah and Reuben, since his wife died in childbirth thirty years earlier. Ezekiel was the proprietor of the general store, located a thousand yards westward along the Boston Post Road from their home.

The father, Reuben, who was more robust than Ezekiel although he was seventy-six, still spent most days cutting timber for the sawmill. Hannah, dutiful mother and wife, was happiest staying at the house performing the chores necessary to keep the three of them healthy and warm.

They were regular and active members of the two-story wooden-frame church next to the common at the south end of the Durham Road. They had never worshipped in any other church. It was the only church in the village, and the Hutchins did not travel to the nearby towns along the coastline.

Ezekiel had been baptized in the meeting house and had spent almost every Sabbath since then at worship. The meeting house had been constructed in 1743, using many of the beams and timber from the first structure erected thirty-six years earlier. Having been born in 1746, Ezekiel could not remember any other meeting house. He had been married there and, too soon afterward, had attended the funeral of his wife and first-born child.

The drum had called the congregation to the funeral service, and the muffled beating remained in Ezekiel's memory. The drum gave him many more memories as he lived less in the present and more in the past as he grew older.

When Ezekiel was fifty-three, the ecclesiastical society members voted to build a tower on the west end of the meeting house. At a later meeting, there was a discussion that led to the proposal that a new bell should be purchased by the church and mounted in the tower. The meeting house was filled with almost all those eligible to vote. After several speakers had indicated good reasons for the purchase of a church bell, Ezekiel stood up and spoke.

"My friends, I ask that each of you consider carefully the future meaning of this proposal. You are considering an action which would eliminate one of our best traditions. I looked up in the clerk's records to find this information: 'At a meeting held in December 1714, John Grave was chosen to beat the drum on Sabbath days and other publick days for twenty shilling a year.' For almost as long as our church has existed, we have had a cherished tradition of the drum, which sends out the message of every worship service and meeting. Our grandparents and parents have come in response to the drum. Why should we change this tradition simply because someone has made such a suggestion?"

Pastor John Elliott, tall and lean with long, dark hair, raised his hand to interrupt Ezekiel's remarks. He inquired: "Ezekiel, what is your real objection to a bell? Is it only that you support the tradition of the drum?"

He shook his head, saying: "Pastor Elliott, I have several good reasons. One of them is that our own faithful member, Solomon, would be without his special task as our drummer. For many years he has served so well and joyfully. If we voted to replace the drum with a bell, you would be removing a responsibility from Solomon that he would rather continue. He has no other desire in life but to be our drummer. This is his godly vocation."

"Ezekiel, surely the Lord will find another task for him. Or, perhaps Solomon deserves some well-earned rest in his final years of life," the young pastor responded.

"But pastor, Solomon is not strong enough to become a bell-ringer. He is not able to learn a new skill. If you should decide to buy a bell and put the drum away, I will grieve for my friend Solomon."

"My dear brother, we will find some way to take care of Solomon. If we do that, will you be able to support buying a bell?"

"No, I am afraid not. I have another reason to keep the drum. It is a reason of the heart. The drum beats remind me regularly of my youth, especially when my wife and I attended church together. My memories are my biggest reasons for opposing a bell."

The pastor responded to Ezekiel: "You are a good storekeeper, the best we have in town. Certainly, you should realize the value of a new bell to attract people to worship. In your store, you do not keep in stock all the old items which are no longer popular. It is the same in the church. If it is now popular to have a bell, and the members of the ecclesiastical society vote for it, you would not oppose it then, would you?"

Ezekiel slowly scanned the eyes of his neighbors watching him. He tightened his grip on the back of the pew. "I believe in majority rule. I would have to abide by the vote of the majority." Then, his argument finished, he sat down beside his father.

Pastor Elliott continued speaking to Ezekiel: "A bell would not take away your precious and happy memories. In fact, it may help you live more in the present, rather than so much in the past."

The discussion among the men and women continued for another hour. Almost all of the speakers were in support of the bell. The time for the vote came, and only three people voted against the purchase: Ezekiel, Reuben, and Hannah Hutchins. His parents had been quiet during the discussion. Their vote was an overt indication of their support for his views.

As they were leaving the meeting house, Ezekiel spoke sadly to his parents: "I resolve never again to set foot inside this building. I must live by my principles. It would be against the blessed memory of my wife if I were to continue to remain in fellowship with these folk."

Ezekiel Hutchins kept his word. For more than one year, he attended neither worship services nor public meetings. He continued to work hard in his store.

On a bright April afternoon, he was checking the inventory on his shelves. A stranger entered the store. She was well-dressed, wearing a long black gown and a tight black bonnet. A few wisps of gray hair peeked from the bonnet's edges. Judging from the time of day, Ezekiel surmised she must have arrived on the stage from New Haven en route to Boston.

Always ready to assist a customer, Ezekiel smiled, tipped his head, and declared: "Good afternoon, madam. May I help you?"

"Yes, sir, perhaps you could. I have come to oversee the delivery of a bell for the East Guilford meeting house."

Ezekiel's eyes squinted, his forehead furrowed. "Oh?"

She continued: "I represent the company that cast the bell. I escorted the bell to the ship in New York where it was loaded to come to East Guilford. However, the crew at the ship would not permit me to travel as a passenger on board ship."

Ezekiel replied: "It can sometimes be a rough trip if there is a spring storm. A cargo ship is not the best means of transportation for a lady such as yourself."

"Well, sir, I have a responsibility to my customers to make certain that there is no damage done to the bell in transit. I would like to be at the dock in town when it is unloaded."

"Certainly, madam. The ship has probably already arrived at the East Wharf. Young Philander, who should be working out back in the powder house, would be able and willing to drive you by wagon down to the dock."

"That would be fine. Thank you for your help."

The woman turned, hesitated, and stepped back toward the counter. "One other thing. I plan to stay here a few days. Could you recommend a hospitable lodging?"

Ezekiel scratched his head, then asserted: "My highest recommendation would be Miss Florence's. Again, after you have overseen the unloading at the dock, Philander could take you over there at your convenience."

The woman raised her eyebrows in delight and replied: "That sounds perfectly wonderful. Thank you."

"I could notify her in advance that you will be arriving. Whom should I say that she will be expecting?"

"Please tell Miss Florence that the Widow Charpentier will be most delighted to rest at her lodgings. Thank you. Good day."

She briskly stepped out the door. Ezekiel paused a brief moment. Then he resumed his work sorting the shelves.

Fairly soon, Philander drove his horse and wagon down to the East Wharf with his solitary passenger. Having ascertained her purpose in town, Philander cheerfully declared: "This new bell of yours has been anticipated for months by most of the folks in our town. Today is a special day with its arrival. Personally, I can hardly wait until it is installed and can be heard across the common."

The Widow Charpentier replied, "I am pleased to hear that."

Philander snapped the whip briskly, saying, "There is only one person in all of East Guilford who is against your bell."

"Truly, who could that be?"

"Old Mr. Hutchins. The gentleman who runs the store you came from."

"I find that hard to believe. He seemed to be such a charming and considerate gentleman."

"Perhaps that is your first impression. But he is very much opposed to the bell. He has not been inside the meeting house since the congregation decided to place an order for a bell."

"It appears that he is quite an adamant person."

"Well, he has his definite reasons. It does seem that a man should be able to get over past events and begin a new life."

At that moment, Philander pulled up on the reins. They had reached the wharfside. He assisted the widow from his wagon. Immediately their conversation ended, as she began talking with the ship's crew.

About noon the next day, a large crowd gathered at the meeting house to watch the bell as it was hoisted by ropes and pulleys into the tower. It was a festive moment for the men, women and, especially, the children. The academy schoolmaster dismissed the children from school for the day. He said: "They won't be paying attention to their lessons anyway. They might as well learn firsthand about the application of some of Newton's laws."

Solomon struck the drum with a roll and flourish for the last time. Then he carried it over to Ezekiel's store. From inside the front doorway, the two of them watched the festivities. If a customer approached the store, they quickly pretended that they were occupied inside, totally disregarding the community event. Although the celebration was taking place a few hundred feet from the store, this was a routine day of business, or so they made it appear.

The next few months of a humid and hot summer passed quickly. Some of the villagers described the events of a new awakening of the Holy Spirit within the church and the community. Many more people attended services. Several made new commitments to serve the Lord.

One of the new members that summer was the Widow Charpentier. She had decided that it was time to retire from work as a representative of the foundry. She decided that East Guilford was a pleasant village in which to settle. She often came to Ezekiel's store for purchases but, as far as anyone heard, the bell was never mentioned by either one of them.

On a cool, clear day in early November, Reuben Hutchins, Ezekiel's father, went out at dawn to fell some timber. All the leaves had fallen from the trees. It was a good season to prepare some timber for the mill. Shortly after noon on that same day, Philander came running into the store.

"Mr. Hutchins! Mr. Hutchins! Your mother wants you to come to the house right away. She is mighty upset about something! You go. I'll look after the store."

"Thanks, Philander. I'm going."

As quickly as he could, Ezekiel rushed down the street. He found his mother in the kitchen, sitting at the table, appearing distraught. She stood up as he came toward her, placing his hands on her shoulders.

"What is the matter, Ma?"

"Zeke, I am sorry to disturb you at work. But I have a terrible feeling that something has happened to your father. He said that he would be back around noon. It is past four o'clock."

"Yes. He usually works only half the day. I will go out and find him. Don't you worry. Maybe something is wrong with the horse."

"No, Zeke. I don't believe that it is Nellie. I believe that he has been hurt. I just know it."

"All right, Mother. Let me get some help from the neighbors. Levi Ward and his two sons might be able to go with me."

Not listening to him, Hannah shook her head from side to side, muttering to herself. "I told him. I told him that he is getting too old to work on the trail all by himself. He says everything is all right, that the exercise is good for him. Why do I listen to him? Oh, Reuben, my dear Reuben!" She began to sob. Ezekiel put his arms around her shoulders, reassuring her.

"Calm down, Mother. He will be found. There is probably nothing wrong. Don't get so disturbed."

Ezekiel sat down by the iron stove. He took off his store shoes and replaced them with his boots. He put on a heavier coat and hat. He took the lantern from the wall.

He stepped out the back door toward the barn. After saddling his horse, he rode quickly over to the Ward farmhouse.

Levi Ward was fifty years old. His two grown sons worked in their apple orchard together. After Ezekiel explained the situation quickly, Levi suggested another idea. It might take the four of them several hours to locate Reuben. Levi Ward was one of the two deacons of the church. His first idea was to seek more help.

"Listen, Ezekiel. If we call together all of the able-bodied men in the village, we will have a better chance of finding your father. It could take hours to locate him. Let me get some more help."

Before Ezekiel could agree with Levi, he was following the deacon across the yard to the common. Hastily, he followed Levi right into the east doorway of the meeting house without realizing where he had gone.

Levi looked up at the rope hanging in the hall and declared, "Let's ring the alarm!"

He began pulling down on the rope, then letting it pull him up with a hard, abrupt tug. Immediately, Ezekiel heard the bell pealing above him. Levi continued to pull up and down, up and down, up and down. Soon it appeared as if the bell was doing the work of pulling Levi up and down, as the rhythm of pealing was established. The exertion began to show as Levi's face became red and he began to breathe heavily.

Ezekiel declared, "Let me take over for you." He stepped into place, nudging Levi to the side, following the pattern already begun. Long pulls downward, then a quick return as the bell turned and rang, beginning another peal.

Usually, the bell had sounded steadily and slower when it was rung for worship. A few times, it had been rung strongly and rapidly, for certain emergencies. This was clearly an alarm.

Within a few minutes, several men arrived at the meeting house. In another fifteen minutes, about fifty men and women, plus several children, gathered inside the building. Ezekiel recognized neighbors and friends who came from as far away as the Neck district to the west and from the Hammonasset River to the east. All of them were his customers. They were also members of the church.

For the past six months, Ezekiel had seen them in various places, including his store, but not within the meeting house since his self-imposed absence. Several of them sat in the pews and benches along the walls. Others stood in smaller groups at the doorways.

Pastor John Elliott stood up beside the communion table below the high pulpit. He had been their pastor for almost four years. Ezekiel stood beside the young pastor. Deacon Ward and Deacon Timothy Hill sat in their deacon's chairs on either side of the table. Ezekiel appeared uneasy because of his long absence from participating in the Lord's Supper and regular worship. He had chosen not to enter this building on this, or any other, account.

Robert Loesch

Once the crowd had gathered, Ezekiel began to speak. "Friends, my father is missing out in the woods above the hunter's trail. He did not come back from working as he usually does at the noon hour. We do not have much time before it becomes dark. I would be most grateful if some of you could come with me to search for him. It is possible that he has been hurt."

Pastor Elliott looked over at Ezekiel, placed his hand on the old man's forearm, and spoke to the gathering: "Let us divide ourselves into teams of five men each. All of us can go up the Durham Road. Then we can split to search in different sections of the woods. That way we will not waste time covering the same territory. Quickly, let us go!"

Deacon Hill, too weak himself to join the search, raised his hand to hush the noise of the crowd. He looked up at the pastor, saying, "Aye, but before we go, please may we offer a word of prayer for a safe deliverance?"

"Yes, thank you, Deacon Hill. Let us all pray: O Lord God Almighty, who wast able to lead thy people through the wilderness of Egypt for forty years in search of thy Promised Land, be with us now in this day as we go into this wilderness in search of one of thy faithful followers, good Reuben Hutchins. As Thou hast called us to this place for worship of thy Holy Name, let thy guidance direct us to find Reuben. By your presence and everlasting mercy, we pray. Amen."

A resounding "amen" arose from the men and women. Then, without further directions, they rushed out onto the common. Several went with horses and wagons. Others walked. Most of the groups carried lanterns in preparation for the approaching dusk.

For the next few hours, the various teams walked through the woods. Each one called out: "Reuben! Where are you?" or "Mr. Hutchins, can you hear us?" or "We are coming!"

After each call, the men would allow an interval in which they waited for a response. But for hours, no one heard a reply, only the calls in the darkness.

Although there were some trails to follow, there were also rocky ledges and swamps off the trails that were investigated. Each area of evergreens and dense underbrush was also checked carefully.

About nine o'clock, long after the sun had set, one of the teams called out. "There he is. We have found him!"

At first the lanterns shone upon his horse and wagon. Some fifty feet away, they found an unconscious body underneath a fallen tree.

"Now be very careful with him."

"He is not awake. But he is still breathing."

8

"Thank the Lord!"

"We must first lift the tree from him. You, and you, as we lift up, drag him from under it."

The five men, with great effort, lifted the tree and moved him to safety. Carefully, they lifted his limp body up into his wagon. They brought the wagon and horse, with its passenger, slowly down the trail and onto the road. They brought him back to the Hutchins' house.

The doctor came quickly and examined Reuben. After more than an hour with him, the doctor asked to speak with Hannah. By this time, Ezekiel had come back to the house with his own team of searchers. Many of the other men were still in the woods. There was no way they could have known that Reuben had been found. Some others returned to their own homes in order to wait until the early morning when the search would be easier.

From within their kitchen, Ezekiel heard the meeting house bell. Again, it was the alarm call for a meeting.

The doctor turned to Ezekiel and suggested: "You should go over and report to them the news. The alarm will bring in the men still in the woods. It will report the end of the search."

"Yes, thank you, doctor."

Ezekiel went directly to the meeting house. For the second time that day, he entered the building with the bell. Again, many of his friends were there. He was told that some of them, unable to search, had stayed there to pray for his father.

He went to the platform below the pulpit.

"I have come straight from my house. My father has been found. He is awake. The doctor says that he should live. He has a badly broken leg and several broken ribs. With the loving care of my mother, he should survive and be restored to good health. I ... I am deeply grateful for what each of you has done for us. I wish to offer a word of thanksgiving. Let us bow before God our Maker.

"Almighty and Most Merciful God, I thank Thee. We thank Thee for thy special mercies this day. We give Thee thanks for guiding us to my father's side, and for bringing him home safe and alive. We give Thee thanks for our friends who came together to help find him.

"But most of all, dear Lord, I thank Thee for thy voice which called us to this place of worship. Thanks be to Thee for thy voice, the bell. Forgive me that I did not want to give up the drum. Now I know, heavenly Father, that this bell has a much stronger and clearer voice when help is sorely needed.

For thy voice, this bell, I thank Thee. In the name of Jesus Christ, Our Lord. Amen."

In hushed unison, the congregation uttered in reply, "Amen." One man whispered, "That was a most beautiful prayer." His neighbor replied, "Yes, and more than one miracle was performed this day for which we can give thanks."

It was a while before Ezekiel could return to his house. Many of his neighbors wanted to visit with him in the meeting house about the day's events.

Two months later, on the first day of January, the bell pealed joyously again. This time, it called the people into the meeting house where the Widow Charpentier and Ezekiel Hutchins were joined together in holy matrimony.

George Hendee – Bicycle Champion

Springfield, Massachusetts, 1882

George Hendee, my good friend, disappeared without a trace the day after he won four first prizes in the bicycle races in New Haven, Connecticut. On October 5, 1882, he had come out of nowhere, so to speak, a young man just barely sixteen years old from Springfield. He was not one of the well-known, popular young Yale men in the races.

We had traveled down together from Springfield to New Haven. We stayed overnight at the YMCA just off the Yale campus. We barely had enough money to pay for our room. For lunch, we had a hot dog at the street cart on Chapel Street. This was an adventure for both of us.

George's brother lived in New Haven, and George had come to visit the city before. But this was his first appearance in the popular high-wheel bicycle races. As his assistant, I would hold his bike steady as he mounted it and while waiting for the starting gun to be fired.

As we were walking along the city streets that day before the races, George said to me, "David, don't act like we are country bumpkins among all these university fellows."

"So I should stop chewing on straw?" I replied.

"Just act as if we are smart and sophisticated. That is how they act all the time."

In a few moments, a group of Yalies jeered at us. One of them declared: "Where did you buy those clothes? Not in any gentleman's shop, that's for sure."

The next day, while George was racing and I was watching and cheering him along the sidelines, the antagonism toward him was downright vehement. The crowds clearly favored the Yale cyclists—and disfavored anyone else. Between heats, most of these university men were surrounded by beautiful young women from the town. One of the cyclists had tied a bright scarf on his handlebars. He looked like a knight in a medieval tournament with his maiden's ensign.

In contrast, I was George's only cheering section. I'm not quite as appealing to the eye. I am good looking in a rough kind of way. At one place along the route, I saw two students attempt to unbalance George by rolling stones under his big wheel. At another point, one of the competitors tried to ram George's bicycle to push him out of the running. Not only were these attempts unsportsmanlike, they were very dangerous. A fall from the high seat can cause a great deal of damage.

But George persevered. He ignored the taunts of the crowd. He focused on each race.

On that day, October 5, he won the half-mile race, the half-mile without hands, the slow race, and the five-mile race. "By George, George," I exclaimed. "You won four top prizes in one day!"

What was amazing was that he had first ridden a bicycle only eleven months earlier. A few days after that first time, he rode on a high-wheel bicycle from Springfield to his uncle's home, thirty miles away. He had ridden the sixty-eight miles down to visit his brother in New Haven on a 48-inch standard Columbia bicycle in fourteen hours. Then had constructed his own high-wheel machine from a carriage wheel, a gas pipe, and a small wheel.

In April of 1882, he had won a fancy-riding contest in his hometown. Three months later, on July 4, he won his first race in Springfield, pedaling two miles.

The day after his four-prize victory in New Haven, he had disappeared. He had not given me any clues as to what he was going to do on October 6. I assumed that we would be returning home together. My first fear was that some local ruffians, jealous because he had whipped the Yale riders, had beaten him up. I checked at the local police department and in the hospital, but there was no evidence that he had been brought to either place. George's brother had heard nothing from him either.

The police officers advised me to return to Springfield. I gave them my address. They assured me that they would notify me when he was found. They were certain that he was safe and told me not to worry.

On my train ride back to Springfield, I thought about our friendship. George and I had worked together at C.E Seymour and Company, Hack, Livery, Boarding and Sale Stables at 65 Market Street. George had developed firm, lean muscles from repairing carriage wheels. Both of us worked six days a week, every day after school and all day on Saturdays. My job was grooming the horses in the stables on the first floor.

That very year, we had helped in the move of the stables from the former Massasoit Stables location to the new three-story brick building. The first floor held sixty horses. There were 125 carriages stored on the second and third floors. First-class single- and double-horse teams were available for drives. It was a growing business. It was hard work, but we enjoyed every day.

As I arrived back at the train station, I thought especially about Sundays. George considered Sunday to be the best day of the week. He could drive one of the Seymour carriages for one of the families wishing to go for a Sunday drive. These leisurely drives often took most of the afternoon.

George often drove carriages for some of the families living in the new McKnight neighborhood, with its beautiful and ornate houses. This was how George met Nancy Harrison, the daughter of one of the families for whom he was the hired driver. She was two years younger than he. If he wanted to spend any time with her, he had to have a chaperone, usually one of her parents or another older woman. Although I had offered, I was never considered for a chaperone.

When I got home, I went to Nancy's home to inform her that George was missing in New Haven. She cried and then became angry. "How could you have left there without knowing what had happened to him?"

"The police assured me that they would look for him and that they would make sure he came back safely."

"David," she protested, "what if he is lying in a ditch somewhere wounded? What if he is wandering around not knowing who he is? You should have stayed there until you found him."

"But Nancy, I trusted the police officer's promises. Besides, if neither of us came back to work for Mr. Seymour, we could both lose our jobs."

We worried for two more days. George returned, without any advance notice, unscathed, on the New York, New Haven, and Hartford Railroad. Soon after, we met at my house, shook hands, and embraced. He looked great. Then after I scolded him for not sending a telegram indicating that he was safe, he told me what had happened.

"David, you will never believe this story. A man invited me to stay with him for the last couple of days. This was no ordinary man. He is the director of athletics at Yale. He had seen how I had been reviled and scorned by the local people, especially by the university students themselves."

I replied: "There's no doubt that you were treated unfairly, my friend. I am glad someone there sought to make amends to you."

He continued: "There's even more. But I can't tell you. The stranger told me, 'Keep this under your hat.' We made a gentleman's agreement, his word and mine."

I declared, putting my hand over my heart, "I swear that your secret will be safe with me."

"No, David, a man's word is his bond. I won't even tell Nancy until the time is right. I will tip my hat to her, as a lady, but I won't let the secret come out."

For the rest of the year and into 1883, George and I continued to work at the Seymour stables. The friendship between George and Nancy continued to grow. George volunteered for as much extra work as he could get. He told me he was saving his funds for "something special."

During the racing season, in the fall and then in the spring, George entered as many races as he could. I still went as his assistant. But now, Nancy joined us, along with her mother or father. We went to bicycle races in Mott Haven, New York; the American Institute in Boston; Harvard; Worcester; and Albany. On race day, we hitched his bicycle to the back of the railroad car or stored it in the baggage car.

In June, George won the one-mile championship in Mott Haven. The following September, he won the ten-mile race in Springfield. The newspapers were enthralled by his achievements. He was becoming a sports celebrity. Besides his sporting skill, he was dashing in appearance. He was five foot ten inches tall and 176 pounds, with light brown hair. He was seen as a clean-cut boy. He was temperate and did not engage in smoking, chewing, or drinking.

By the time George was seventeen, in October 1883, he told me: "You can put this in your pipe and smoke it. I will have my response to those Yale men who scorned me last year as an outsider."

Because I didn't smoke either, I knew he was only using the familiar expression. I declared: "I am sure of that. You will win again."

"No, David, even more. It is time to tell you my secret. I have been able to complete my agreement with the director of athletics at Yale. He promised me that if I could save enough money for the first year of tuition at Yale, he would provide me a room to stay in his house as a freshman. He also promised me financial aid for my meals. When I have finished my high school studies here, I will be able to enroll as a Yale student."

"That's great. What a secret! You will be an honor to Springfield and to all of your friends here." We hugged and jumped up and down in glee.

The next time we went to New Haven to race on the high-wheeler, George was ready. Nancy and her parents rode with us. This time George brought his own cheering section.

He took the races like a storm that came out of nowhere. Nancy's blue scarf was flying from the handlebars as he crossed the finish line for each victory. Quite a day! And quite a knight!

Natasha's Epiphany Gift

Novgorod, Russia, 1987

Natasha's dark brown eyes sparkled with excitement. She was looking forward to showing her new American friend the old section of her hometown, Novgorod, Russia.

Twenty-one years old, she lived with her parents and brothers in an apartment a few blocks from the red-brick walled "kremlin," or "old city."

Natasha had met George the day before while he was visiting the city for a few days. George's father managed a small corporation in the import-export business in Moscow. George was a first-year university student, also in Moscow, among a group of international students studying in English-speaking classes.

Natasha and George had agreed to meet at ten o'clock at the main gate into the kremlin so that she could show him some of the old buildings.

As a tall, lean, blond young man came around the corner, she heard his cheery greeting: "Good morning! I hope you have not been waiting too long. It is cold today!"

She smiled and replied: "Nyet. Not at all! I am happy to see you."

George said: "We only have a few hours to explore before I need to get back to the hotel and make the train back. So let's get going."

She was bundled in a dark brown fur-trimmed coat that reached her ankles. Her black hair peeked from the edges of her bright red hat.

"First, let us go look across the river from the walls."

They turned and walked through the gate onto the stone walkway. It was a bitter cold January day. The wind was blowing across the open space. Some snow blew from the drifting piles across the walk.

Natasha looked up at George and declared: "I hope that you understand my English. I have been studying several years in school. I always try to listen when visitors come here. There is so much to learn."

"You speak very well. And I'm glad that you do. I don't speak much Russian at all. Next semester, I plan to start formal language studies. How old is Novgorod?"

"This is one of the oldest cities of Russia. It became an independent city able to govern itself in 1136," she began.

"Eleven hundred and thirty-six? That is incredible! That is more than eight hundred and fifty years old," George exclaimed with astonishment.

She continued: "Novgorod was the capital of all northern Russia, all the way to the Ural Mountains. During the Middle Ages, it was very famous as an important business and cultural center."

George noticed five large bronze bells mounted on a cement foundation alongside each other on the ground. Looking up, he could see the empty bell tower where they had once hung. He could almost imagine what it must have sounded like to hear them ringing across the city.

They walked through a passage that opened out into a view of the outer kremlin walls and the river.

Natasha pointed. "See? Across the Volkhov River you can see the other half of the old city. On that side was the commercial center where the merchants had their shops. On this side was the center for religious and political life. During the twelfth century, Novgorod was one of the four trade centers of the Hanseatic League."

George asked, "What were the other major cities in the league?"

"Bergen, Norway; London, England; and Bruges, Belgium."

George replied: "My father would be interested in that. He is a strong believer in the value of international trade. I never thought of him as belonging to a long, venerable tradition of business merchants."

"Today," she continued, "Novgorod is most famous for her ancient history and her old buildings, including many churches. But with the changing times, and the improved relations between Russia and America, Novgorod is again becoming famous as a modern city."

Natasha pulled her coat collar closer around her neck to keep out the cold wind. Each time she spoke, her breath crystallized into frosty white air.

For a long time, they stood talking about Novgorod, the Volkhov, and their long history.

A young family of three children and their parents walked by, laughing and skipping. Soon, an elderly couple slowly passed them. George and Natasha looked at each other. George said, "It seems that both the young and the old enjoy your city."

Natasha replied: "That is true. This is a wonderful place to live."

After a while, they turned around and walked back into the open square of the kremlin.

As they did, George noticed a large white building dominating the sky to the right, inside the walls. It had five gold domes on its roof, shining brightly against the dark gray sky.

He pointed up and asked, "What is that building?"

"That is the Cathedral of Saint Sophia, the most important church in our whole city. Would you like to see it? I know that it is open because today is a religious holy day." He nodded in agreement. They walked into the churchyard and around to the entrance.

Before they entered, Natasha paused by the large bronze doors, covered with many scenes. "These doors were made in Magdeburg, Germany, in the twelfth century. Look here. Down in this corner you can see the portraits of two German artisans who made the doors, with a Russian figure between them."

For almost twenty minutes, they admired the twenty-six panels, each depicting a story from the Bible. Natasha knew each story and made the engraved figures on each panel come alive.

Finally, they stepped into the darkness of the sanctuary. Immediately, sheltered from the snowy blast, they became warmer. As she loosened her coat and stomped the snow off her boots, he did likewise.

A friendly elderly woman nodded and smiled at them as they caught their breaths. Natasha spoke a few words in Russian to the woman.

Natasha turned to George, "She says that you are a good-looking stranger."

"And what did you say to her?" George inquired.

"I told her that I agreed with her," Natasha replied, with her eyes shyly looking down toward the floor.

"How did she know I was a stranger?"

"Your clothes are American. Besides, she has never seen you here before," Natasha answered.

"Well, I feel very welcome here. And thanks for the compliment."

"You are welcome … This is my church. It is open during the week as a museum for visitors. But, for me, it is also the place where I come to worship. In recent years, we have been allowed to worship here more often. For many years, the government allowed us to worship here only on special holy days."

George looked around the interior, awed by the beauty and the stillness. He asked, "Why are the candles all lit?"

"Remember? I told you that today is a religious holy day. This is January sixth, the Feast of the Epiphany. This is the day when we celebrate the birth of Jesus Christ."

George frowned. Puzzled, he asked, "But don't you celebrate Christmas on December twenty-fifth like we do in America?"

Natasha understood his dismay. She replied: "In the Russian Orthodox Church, and in all Eastern Orthodox traditions all over the world, Epiphany is celebrated as the true day when Jesus was recognized as the Savior of the whole world. It was on the Twelfth Night, January sixth, when the Wise Men came from the East bringing their gifts. This was when those beyond his own country accepted him as their messiah."

George looked at her, seeming to be satisfied with her explanation. "I think I understand."

She continued: "Epiphany means … how would you say it? A revelation, a manifestation. It is the time when God revealed Himself to the world, to the Gentiles. It is more important than the birth itself. Also on Epiphany, we remember the baptism of Jesus when he was an adult, another time when who He was became revealed to people."

"Do you give gifts at Epiphany then?"

"Oh, yes," Natasha replied. "We remember that the Wise Men brought gifts to the infant. So we give gifts to each other because of this great, wonderful gift to all of us."

George looked around, his eyes finally adjusted to the darkness. He could see paintings hanging on the tall wooden wall at the front of the church. "What are all those paintings?" he asked.

"Icons. They are paintings on wood, showing different leaders in the Bible or in the history of the church. Some are prophets and apostles, others are martyrs and saints."

She told George about some of the icons, showing great familiarity with the lives and stories of her faith.

"Many of the icons were stolen or destroyed during the Great Patriotic War in the nineteen forties. The troops destroyed many of the churches and buildings in our cities. In recent years, many other icons have been brought here to replace those which were lost. Several artists have restored the church to its original beauty. Look up there!"

She pointed to the high ceiling under the central dome.

"That fresco was painted on the ceiling and shows the prophets and the angels. It was painted in the twelfth century, when the cathedral was first built."

George whistled softly. "Wow. Everything around here is so old. The paintings, the church, the city. Over eight hundred years old. In America, something that is two hundred years old is considered very old. But eight hundred years!"

"Yes. Russia has a long history as a civilization. And the Christian religion has been an important part of that history. It has only been since the revolution of 1917 that Christianity had been restricted. But there remained many people who continued to believe and practice their faith. The increase of our rights has encouraged the renewal of Russian religious life as well as many other freedoms among our people."

"I am glad to learn about all of this," George exclaimed.

"Even the son of an American businessman has much to learn about our people and our culture. I am glad that I can be your guide to help you."

George smiled at her friendly criticism. "And there is much that Russians are learning about the United States. I am glad that we have started a friendship. We can learn from each other. Our two governments are working to cooperate in many major ways in the last decades. There is also the need for cooperation and understanding among individuals of our two countries. As two individuals, we can help build such understanding."

Natasha nodded affirmatively and stated: "Good. The main reason I have been studying English is so that I can work someday as an interpreter. I think each person can find some personal ways to increase our knowledge about each other's culture."

George looked at his watch and quickly asserted: "Oh no. I have to leave now. I wish the time had not passed so fast. Maybe we can see each other again when I can return to Novgorod. Let me give you my address in Moscow, and we can write each other."

Natasha replied, "Fine. Let me give you mine, too." She took a card and pen from her purse and began to write. George wrote on a piece of notepaper.

He looked around at the cathedral walls once more. The beauty of the frescoes and the icons, the stillness of the sanctuary, filled him with joy. He had learned so much today and had so much more to learn.

They exchanged their notes. Seeing a message in Russian, George asked, "What else did you write?"

He looked at the Russian lettering, which meant nothing to him.

"It is my Epiphany greeting to you. It says, 'Peace on earth, good will among men.'"

"Wonderful," George replied. "Thank you. That is a special gift. To me and all people everywhere."

He extended his hand for a handshake. She put her arms around his shoulders and gave him a hug. Then he said: "Don't forget to write. Goodbye, and keep studying."

He wrapped his coat tightly around his chin and stepped out from the church. Back in the cold air, he started to run toward the main gate.

Six Candles

Village on the road to Leningrad (St. Petersburg), Russia, 1987

My name is Masha Rublev. I am the widow of Alexander Rublev. I wish to tell you about one special day this past summer when I spoke slowly and sadly to my lovely granddaughter. "Valentina, these days have gone by so quickly. It hardly seems that a week has already gone past."

The young girl stopped, leaned on the pitchfork, and replied: "That's true, Grandma. I wish that tomorrow would not come. I am not ready to go back to Leningrad and school."

Valentina has always loved her visits with me in the countryside, I thought to myself. *For all of her sixteen years, she has lived in a city apartment. Yet, she has managed to visit me almost every summer. This week I have been taking care of her while her mother is on vacation with her fellow workers in Repino.*

"You know, Valentina, you are a great help to me in doing the chores. Now that I am eighty-eight, it is not easy to take care of my little *izba* and the yard all alone."

I realized that she loves more than the green grass, the trees, and the good folk of our village. This is also the birthplace of her father, Peter. Perhaps she thinks about him when she is here. Six years ago he was arrested, convicted, and imprisoned. Neither Valentina, nor her mother, nor I have heard about him during that time. Both of Valentina's older brothers are away from home in the army. I am pleased that she chose to stay with me during the week that her mother was on vacation. Especially now that she has become old enough to make her own decisions.

I swept the hair back from my brow, wiping the moisture off my face with my sleeves. I declared: "Well now, all of the yard is hayed. We have done a good day's work. Let us rest a bit before supper." We placed our tools, the pitchfork, and the scythe against the side of the *izba*. Then we sat down upon the single step leading into the front door of my home.

Immediately, Valentina began. "Grandma, tell me about Grandpa Rublev! You always like to tell stories about him."

"Yes, my dearest one! He would have loved to have known you. You are so much like your father. You always want to know about people, what they are doing and thinking."

I began to think about Peter but then remembered that she had asked about her grandfather, not her father. *Later*, I thought, *I will tell her about her father*. "Yes, Alexander Rublev, your grandfather, was a kind young man. He was tall and dark-haired, powerful in his body and his mind.

"We both went to school together, although he was a few years older than I. One evening, as we were walking along the river, he asked me to become his bride. Dearest Alexander, he loved to walk along the river that continues to flow through our village. We agreed that we would always live near a river. We planned the house that we built together so that it was overlooking the flowing water. We loved to watch the small boats cruise by, to fish, to enjoy the activities along the banks. We also enjoyed the cool breeze in the evenings and to see the changing seasons alter the character of the life-giving, softly moving stream."

My teenage listener interrupted. "Grandma, Babushka, this week I have been talking with the other young people in the village who gather down by the river. Boys and girls still meet and share their dreams of a future together, just like you and Grandpa did."

"That is true; that does not change. There will always be a future and hope in a world where there are young people sharing their dreams together … " Again, I began to drift away, recalling my own plans with Alexander. Valentina touched me lightly on the arm, bringing me back to our conversation.

"Anyway, after a year's engagement, Alexander and I were married in January of 1916. The ceremony took place in the Church of St. Anthony at the center of the old part of the village. I remember clearly to this day the old Orthodox priest. He was wearing his long black robe. Beneath his heavy, reddish-brown beard, which was tinged with some white hairs, he revealed a warmth of love and joy. He offered the blessing of the Church upon us. I remember at the end of the service when the church bells pealed forth so joyfully. We walked together, the three of us, hand in hand, out into the sunlight of the churchyard, surrounded by many friends and family. It was a festive day. Always, the church bells were struck so strongly for a wedding. The bells were the voice of God calling out His blessing upon us."

"Grandma, are you crying because you are so happy?"

I wiped the tears from my cheeks and replied: "Yes and no. I cry also because the bells no longer ring. When I was eighteen, the workers in Petrograd went on strike, and soon there were terrible riots. Back then it was still called St. Petersburg. Shortly, the military garrison in the city joined the workers. Czar Nicholas abdicated his throne when the provisional government was formed.

"It has been years since we have heard the church bells peal. They were removed from the parish belfry more than sixty years ago. The metal was needed, they told us, for making armaments in the factories. They said that the church did not need a bell since the church would soon be closed. It was true. In 1922 the church doors were locked, and services were prohibited. No services have been allowed in our church since that time. But this village was not the only one. Throughout Russia, churches were closed, bells removed, services prohibited, priests taken away and worshippers imprisoned. The sacred objects of brass and silver, such as the candlesticks and icons, were confiscated or destroyed. This was the policy of the state: to encourage atheism and to prevent religious beliefs."

Valentina's jaws clenched tightly. I could see that she had become tense. Then she spoke, not looking directly at me, but toward the street. "But we know that the churches were closed, that all of these things were done, because religion was an evil force. The churches taught superstition and myth. The priests were corrupt. They had become rich from the people's offerings which they used for their own pleasures. The establishment of our Soviet government could not allow such wastefulness and influence to continue!"

I shook my head and said, "How can you say all this?"

But she quickly answered: "It is true. We learn it in school. The churches were closed in order to encourage true patriotism and love of our fatherland."

Sad and astonished at her statements, I replied: "I grieve for what you say. I know that it is taught in the schools. And in the homes and in the newspapers. I have heard those teachings for years from those in authority. I have heard them from your mother, who is such a loyal party member. But why do I need to hear it from you, my dearest one? Why do *you* need to believe the lies and the half-truths of the state? Why do you need to repeat them to me? Why?"

Valentina stood up from the step. She looked around for fear that someone might have heard my words. But no one was within hearing range. Valentina placed her hands on her hips and faced me. "In school, if we say otherwise than what the state teaches us, the soviet of our school meets to discuss and act upon the case. Those who profess to be religious believers, or who are suspected to be believers, are disciplined. They are persecuted harshly. They are punished until they accept the true teaching. Two of my classmates, Ivan and John, were sent away last year to do forced labor as their punishment for being Christians. They are fifteen-year-old criminals, traitors, enemies of the state. Their example and their punishment teaches the rest of us what would happen if we profess any beliefs about God or religion."

"My dear grandchild," I said. I could see that she had learned her lessons well. But she also needed to hear the other side. "My child, Ivan and John are the ones who are standing for the truth, not your classmates, who judge people for having religious beliefs. For centuries, Russia was a Christian nation. Our language, culture, music, art—our entire heritage—is filled with deep Christian meaning. We are a religious people. We always were and always will be. Simply because the teacher teaches one way as the only way does not make it the only way, or the right way, to live. God is, and always will be, the father of our country. Our mother is Holy Russia. To refuse God in our lives is to stand against the solid tradition of our people and our nation."

Valentina protested my statement. She raised her voice and her dark eyebrows. She spoke clearly: "Grandma, you are not at all up to date. I know that you are Christian. But that doesn't mean that I have to be a Christian, too. Stop trying to force your old-fashioned ideas on me."

"I am not forcing any ideas on you. I only want you to know that there is a choice that you can make. There is more than the way of the state … I still believe in God. Your grandfather, Alexander, was an ardent believer. But we are together for such a short time, you and I. Let us not argue on our last evening together. Let us talk about something else."

Although her face was flushed, Valentina shortly calmed down. She said, faintly: "All right. Then tell me more about Grandpa. Please."

She sat down on the freshly cut grass. My bones would not allow me to sit on the ground, so I remained on the front step. From there I could watch some of the children playing across the main highway in front of my house. Across the road, Maria lived with her six children. Until ten years ago it had been a small dirt road that cut through the middle of most of the yards in the village. Now the regular movement of trucks and buses on the wider asphalt highway prevented us from visiting as much as when she first started her family.

"Yes, I will tell you more about your grandfather." I thought that this was why Valentina had always been such a favorite of mine. She often asked to hear about him, whereas no one else in my village wanted me to talk so much about him. I thought about him often, even after so many years, but others have their own interests. Most people, unlike Valentina, do not want to hear an old woman's memories of her life.

So I continued. "Grandpa Alexander worked for more than a year to build this *izba*. The men of the village helped to drag the logs from the woods, but he did the major share of the construction. It remains much as it was when he first finished it except for the little shed on the back. It was almost burned down one year when a kerosene lamp fell to the floor. It is the only house in the entire village which was not destroyed during either of the two great wars. All the rest of the village houses had been burned or bombed during the battles. The church and the school also were spared for use as an infirmary. Josef, a fine local craftsman, carved the fretted eaves along the roof and the carving around the windows."

Valentina looked with pleasure at the intricate, curved woodwork around the windows and under the roof. "Your house comes alive when you talk about its history. It is very special that my grandfather and his friend Josef and his neighbors built it so long ago. So many other houses in the village which were built later look the same. Only this one is my grandfather's." She smiled, and we exchanged nods of agreement.

I continued to reach into the past and share my early life with Valentina. "Our first child was born in this house. He was your father, Peter. I remember the warmth of that day. My labor began late one evening. The air was fresh and smelled sweet but especially since I was ready to give birth. It was a warm and wonderful feeling. I had felt the baby moving quite a bit for a few months, but the immediacy of delivery made all my senses alert. The long wait would soon be over, and our baby would enter the world. The house had been completed during that winter. Alexander and I were looking forward eagerly to start our family."

Valentina asked, "Did you want a boy?"

"Darling, we didn't care whether it was a boy or girl. We only wanted the baby to be healthy. So many children died as infants in those days. We prayed for a healthy child. He was born before the sun came up on the dawn of the thirteenth. My midwife had spent all of the night beside me. Alexander and some of his friends stayed up through the night in the house next door. I felt so alive, so much a part of Mother Earth, when the baby finally came forth and uttered his first cry."

"Did you name him right away, Grandma?"

"Certainly we did. We decided to name him Peter, son of Alexander Rublev. That first afternoon after I had slept deeply for several hours, the priest came to bless him. In a few weeks, Alexander and I took Peter to the Church of St. Anthony to be baptized. This was the same church in which we had been married and where both of my parents had been buried."

Valentina interrupted, "Why did you name my father Peter?"

"Peter was a special name. He was named after St. Peter, the great apostle of our Lord. Although April thirteenth was not the feast day of St. Peter, we wanted him to be our son's patron saint. We wanted our son to be dedicated to service in the Church, as our first-born. Although he did not become a priest and became instead a fine schoolteacher, it was always satisfying that he chose to live in the city of his namesake. One's name helps to shape one's personal destiny in this life."

"You mean when father moved to Leningrad?"

"Yes, but remember that your home city was originally named St. Petersburg."

"Of course, Grandma. The city was founded in 1703 by the command of Peter the Great in order to 'open a window into Europe,'" she recited, as a student would to her teacher.

"Correct. The Fortress of St. Peter and St. Paul was the first building on the Neva River. The city was named first for the Christian saint. Then, in 1914, it was renamed Petrograd after the Russian czar who had built the city. Now, it is called Leningrad in honor of our revolutionary Bolshevik leader." I, too, could show off my knowledge of our country's history.

I stood up and shook off my dress. It was already getting dark as the sun was setting behind the distant forest. It was also becoming quite cool, so I suggested: "Perhaps it is time to go inside. I have a magazine article about your beloved city which I have saved for you. Come in while I try to find it. It is by Alexander Solzhenitsyn, our great contemporary."

We stepped inside the doorway. I placed my arm around Valentina's gentle shoulder for support, but more because the touch was soft and smooth. It was time to begin supper. I suggested that she sit down at the table and read the article aloud to me. That way I could hear the words again. I cannot read very well, and she had been able to read to me during this week. Truly, I regretted that she would be returning home to Leningrad for the fall term tomorrow.

I found the article in my family Bible. "Here it is. He is such a gifted writer. I am glad that he was able to leave Russia safely, although I wish he could have been permitted the opportunity to remain in his homeland. I find so much meaning in what selections of his works that I have been able to hear. My close friends pass along to me copies of what he writes."

Valentina sat down, lit the lamp, and put on her glasses. "Here it begins. He tells about St. Isaac's Cathedral in Leningrad. Listen!"

"'Angels holding candelabra kneel around the Byzantine dome of St. Isaac's.'

"'Three faceted gold spires echo one another across the Neva and the Moika. Everywhere lions, griffins, and sphinxes stand guard over treasure houses, or sleep. History, drawn by her six horses, gallops atop Rossi's ingenious crooked arch. Porticoes by the hundred, thousands of pillars, prancing horses, straining bulls …'

"'What a blessing that no new building was allowed here. No wedding-cake skyscraper may elbow its way onto the Nevsky Prospekt, no five-story shoebox can ruin the Griboyedov Canal. There is no architect living, no matter how servile and incompetent, who can use his influence to build on any site nearer than the Black River or the Okhta.'"

I interrupted her reading, "Isn't that beautiful?"

"Shhh … Solzhenitsyn has more to say yet," the young reader reprimanded me.

"'It is alien to us, yet it is our greatest glory! What a pleasure it is today to stroll down one of those avenues. Yet all this beauty was built by Russians—men who ground their teeth and cursed as they rotted in those dismal swamps. The bones of our forefathers were compressed, petrified, fused into palaces colored ochre, *sang de boeuf*, chocolate brown, green.'

"'And what of our disastrous, chaotic lives? What of our explosions of protest, the groans of men shot by firing squads, the tears of our women: will all this too—terrible thought—be utterly forgotten? Can it, too, give rise to such perfect, everlasting beauty?'"

Valentina put down the paper. "He writes very well. We are not allowed to read anything by him in school. He protests against the government, and they say that he is a poor writer. Frankly, I don't see anything wrong with what he is saying in this piece."

Again, I thought, *she repeats what they teach her in school.* I had to speak. "I have had quite enough of what 'the school' says is good or bad. Solzhenitsyn speaks the truth. We do not forget those who protest for the truth and for freedom. He is a true Russian." I stopped short. I did not want to start another argument with Valentina.

We had been talking before about the birth of Peter. When he had married, he moved to Leningrad. This reminded me of Lenin, so I thought to change the subject. "Valentina, did you know that your grandfather and I also supported Lenin? We were especially proud, particularly your grandfather, that the revolution adopted the hammer and the sickle as its symbol. His two favorite tools were the hammer in building the house and the sickle in working the fields. Together, we supported the rights of the people to lead the government ..."

"Grandma, how could you be a Christian believer and also support the revolution against the czars?"

"It was a hard choice to make. We realized that the czars had become corrupt and autocratic. They no longer knew anything about the real needs of the people. We were sick, starving, and dying. The wealthy rulers did not seem to care. Lenin led the workers to change the government. The trouble is that the new party has also forgotten about the people, while party members gain all the power and wealth. The privileged class of the government officials is no better than the old czarist regime."

"But how can you find that being a Christian is important?"

My Valentina was perceptive and, as with her father, she did not hesitate to ask what was on her mind. I tried to explain my beliefs briefly. "Dear child, we believed that the Church was still important. We knew that it had abused its powers but that religion was an essential part of life. The Soviet constitution declared that citizens had the freedom to have religious beliefs or to be atheists. However, the government policies have advocated atheism and persecuted those who chose to believe in God. I believe modern Christianity and the Soviet government can exist together. Unfortunately, those in power see these as two opposing and incompatible forces. Someday, I truly hope, religious freedom will be upheld in our nation, as the constitution allows."

In the meantime, I had finished preparing dinner. I placed the soup and bowl of potatoes on the table. I poured each of us a cup of milk. During the week, Valentina had seemed satisfied with my cooking. We had shared making meals, and I had taught her some of my special recipes. We enjoyed breaking bread together in our simple, common manner. Now she stated: "You must be careful what you say about your religious beliefs. You could be arrested for some of your statements. I would not want that to happen to you."

I gently answered her fear for my security. "My friends know what I believe. They think that I am harmless. At my age, most people are not going to be influenced by my ideas. I will hardly change my beliefs at this age. I am too old. They think that I am a foolish old woman. Most people ignore me and do not care what I say. You have no reason to worry about my being arrested."

After we had finished supper, Valentina washed out our bowls and spoons. I wiped the table. It was dark enough that I had to light a second lamp.

"Although electricity came to my village ten years ago, I did not see what good it would do. I have been happy without electricity all my life. I told them they can plug my house to anything they want after I am gone but not while I am still alive. They think that I am an old fool on that account too, choosing to live without electrical power. But I see it differently. There are not too many times that we can make decisions, to accept or reject something. We need to use our head when we can decide. I am happier this way."

After a brief pause, I spoke again to Valentina. "I have believed in God all my life. I have not lost my faith. Even when the priests were removed from the village. Even when the church was locked up and all of the beautiful icons were destroyed. Even when the bells were removed from the belfry. Even when the Scriptures were taken away. Through all of that, and more, I still believe in God.

"Even when my Alexander died in the war, I still believed. How else could I continue if I did not believe that God cares for all of us and that there is more to life than the material? God cares for you, too. In my long life, I have seen much that could have made me despair. But my faith has kept me alive. Especially after Alexander died."

"How old was Grandpa when he was killed?"

31

"He was only twenty-five years old. That was in January of 1920, while he was withdrawing with the Bolshevik troops from Latvia. He drowned in the river. So many young men died in all of the wars. So many young women made widows. So many children made orphans ... He died in the river. He loved the river and always wanted to be near the flowing waters of a river. These past sixty years I have stayed in this house, the house that he built, near the river. This was the house of our dreams."

Then Valentina must have remembered her own father who had been born in this house. She asked me, "And when did my father move from here?"

I replied: "Your father ... my son ... lived with me until he was twenty-six. He entered the army to fight against the Germans, and in the summer of 1945 he moved to Leningrad. He had met your mother during the Great Patriotic War, and they helped in the reconstruction of the city. For a few years, two other families lived here with me until more housing was constructed. For the past five years I have been alone again."

"But Grandma, you don't have to stay alone. Mother has invited you to come and live with us in our apartment."

"Yes, I know. That is very kind. But this is my home. This is my village. I have many memories here. The church, the river, my old friends, so much to remember here. It may seem little to you, but it is much to me."

Valentina came over to me and placed her arms around my neck. She drew me close to her, looking into my eyes. "I think I understand now. This week I have learned a lot about life and about you."

I thought that there is still more for her to learn. I suggested: "Before we get ready for bed, let us take a little walk. Tomorrow will come soon, and you will have to return to the city and to school."

As I put on my shawl, I could see the moonlight brighten the corner table by my back window. There were the little toys with which Valentina had played when she came to visit as a child. There was the *matryoshka*, the little wooden nest of dolls, one inside the other, each painted and glazed red and black. For hours, she had played with them, arranging them into different groups or lining up the six of them along the floor. Beside the dolls was the wood carving of the Phoenix, the bird symbolizing hope arising from the ashes. For me this represented how Russia was able to recover its life and its purpose following the massive destruction of the war. The moon was shining brilliantly upon my little silver icon of Christ and St. Peter. Then, there was my white candle for Alexander. As I looked at these objects, small but significant, I began to sing an ancient church melody.

Valentina turned to me, looked gently, and said: "My father used to sing. Mother never sings, but I love to sing."

I said: "Let us go before it is too late. The moon will brighten our path."

Together, we stepped out onto the front walk, a dirt footpath that crossed in front of the house and linked each house along the street. We walked hand in hand toward the older part of the village. Valentina whispered: "You are happy. Where are we going?"

She will soon find out, I thought. I didn't answer her. I said: "Tomorrow is the twenty-fifth of August. Already I have been hearing on my friend's radio announcements for the beginning of school on the first of September. Even at my age I am always reminded that school is part of every child's life. Your vacation is almost over."

I always felt younger, and filled with pride, when I walked out in the village with my special granddaughter. Together, we greeted a few friends who were sitting in front of their own houses. Some of the older boys were out playing ball in the dark. This week with Valentina had gone quickly. I was getting older and yet, as she became older, we had so much more to share this summer. We walked together and worked together as close friends. There was something that she would learn before she went back to the city. My pace began to quicken. She began to hum and move more swiftly. I could not move too quickly, though, because my bones were too stiff.

We went past the home of Nikolai Vachya, and I turned to the left, away from the main footpath and the road. Valentina almost lost her footing as she held onto my arm but continued a step straight ahead.

At this point, we had to go slower. The grass and the bushes were not cut. The moon's light was some help, but the ground was uneven. There were little piles of debris scattered along the side of the narrow path. Some concrete blocks and iron sheets were placed under an apple tree. In another area, the brush had been cut and piled high. It was very quiet. The birds in the trees must have already gone to sleep.

All at once, startling me, Valentina exclaimed: "I know where we are going! There is nothing else this way except the church."

At that moment, we came beyond the trees and could see the belfry of the Church of St. Anthony above us. It was an empty silhouette against the dark sky. The light of the moon reflected off the white plaster tower. The big front doors were surrounded by tall grass and vines. The doors were bolted shut.

Speaking softly I said: "There is a side door that is not locked. Stay close with me." We crept closely around the side of the building. It was difficult moving about and over the piles of assorted junk. For years people had used the churchyard to throw away their refuse. The grass was high and thick, making our steps difficult.

As we came to the side door on the dark side of the church, Valentina declared: "Grandma, we must be careful. The grass here is tramped down. Someone might be hiding inside. Look! There is a beaten-down path leading to the door."

She gripped my arm tightly. "Do not be afraid," I said. "This is a place of peace, not of fear. This is the church were Alexander and I were married. It is where your father was baptized."

"It certainly is quiet—like a cemetery."

I responded: "The souls of the departed are still around us here. You see only signs of death and decay, material artifacts. Only an empty building. And so do most of the people of the village. The party members see this as a completely abandoned building, a symbol of the great destructive might of godless atheism in our village."

We pushed open the door. Its hinges creaked. I entered first, pushing aside some of the cobwebs hanging over the door.

"Be careful, Grandma, please."

"No one is hiding here. Only the souls of the faithful reside here."

Inside, the church was bare. The white stucco walls were cracked in many places. The windows were boarded up. The ceiling was broken and chipped. Large sections of plaster lay on the floor. I remembered the distant past, when the sanctuary was filled with people, the lit candles mounted in front of each icon, the odor of the incense as the priest moved in procession through the gathered congregation. I could recall the chanting of the liturgy.

Valentina broke my silent memories. "I see only an empty, ruined, dusty building. Why do they allow it to remain standing? It has no purpose. You told me that years ago the icons, the cross, the candles, everything had been destroyed or removed. Why do you want to see this?"

"My dearest," I said, pointing toward the darkest corner where the altar had once stood, "there is more to see. Let your eyes adjust more to the darkness." I led her by the arm over to the raised platform.

Seemingly amazed, Valentina whispered, "Someone has been here before us!" There were six candles on the platform, burnt down half their lengths, with wax drippings moving out from the bases like roots from tree trunks. The candles were not lit. Valentina could also see a small bouquet of wildflowers, perhaps a few days since being picked from the fields.

She inquired: "Who has put these here? Are we safe here?"

"Yes, we are safe. We are always safe in the house of God. My sweet one, every Saturday night, past eleven o'clock, a small group of my believer friends and I come here to worship. Every week we worship together; we keep our faith alive. In our homes we have our candles and our separate prayers. But here we worship secretly. We begin our service before midnight and welcome each Sunday morning while everyone else in the village is sleeping."

"But, Grandma, this is illegal! Suppose you were caught during your worship service? You would all be arrested and thrown into prison."

"My dear, we know. We know that very well. But we are not afraid. Every one of us has relatives and friends who are in prison or in labor camps because they are Christians. We have our faith in God's mercy and protection. Nothing can keep us from gathering to give our praise and thanks to Him."

She looked about her and said: "It is so dark. May I light one of these candles?"

"Yes, of course. Here. I have a match."

The room brightened with the flame of the one little candle.

I told her: "Remember that these are candles by which we pray for our loved ones. Do you wish to pray for those you love?"

She hesitated and answered, "I am not yet sure."

That seemed to be the right moment to tell her why I had brought her to the church. "Did you know that you, Valentina, were baptized here?"

"No, not I ... I ... I was never baptized. That would be against the party." Her eyes widened, and her mouth dropped open in amazement.

I continued. "Your father knew that it was against the party. He has never told anyone but the priest and me. He hoped that you would know some day at the right time that you are a baptized Christian. I think that you are old enough now to know this. Even your mother does not know your father's secret about you. I believe that you can be trusted. I know that I can trust you."

Valentina looked as if she did not know what to expect from me next. The knowledge of her baptism seemed enough. Her brows furrowed as she watched me. We stood close to the light of the candle but could not clearly see each other's face. She said: "Are you sure I should know this now? Perhaps it would have been better if I did not know."

35

I declared: "No. The truth is never wrong. You are old enough to know and to make the right decisions as a result of this knowledge." I paused a few moments to be sure that I should continue. I felt sure that this was the best, perhaps the only, moment that I could tell her these things. "Valentina, do you know why your father is in prison? Do you know what he did six years ago that was the cause of his conviction as a criminal?"

"Yes. He was a traitor to the state. My father is an enemy of the people. He met secretly to plot against the government, against the rules which forbid secret gatherings. His crime of treason put him into prison. My mother told me that. That is why she works so hard to be a loyal party member. She must erase the shame that he has brought to us. My teachers have told me that. My friends in school remind me that he is a traitor, but that I can work to overcome his bad name. He is an example of what not to do. Why do you think that I study hard to be a good and obedient student? I, too, must erase by my life what my father did." She began to tremble, thinking about him and the shame and suffering that had been brought upon her family.

I knew the suffering that she had endured, for she had often told me the dreadful stories from school. I, too, began to tremble for her. "My dearest Valentina. This is what everyone has told you for the past six years. It has not been an easy burden. It is not easy to grow up without your father. But has any one every told you the exact details of what your father's crime was?"

"No, only that it was an act of treason and plotting. No one would tell me the details. Not even Mother."

"Tonight, I will tell you."

"Yes. Go on." She looked up, expectantly, with even greater puzzlement.

"Your father, Peter, my son, Peter, and the son of Alexander, committed no crime in the eyes of God but only in the eyes of the state. For his one crime, he was put into prison and, to this day, as far as we know, languishes there. His crime was singing 'alleluia!' and praying during a secret worship service in the forest outside Leningrad. The police arrested the leaders of the secret nighttime gathering. Such meetings are illegal. This was his only 'crime of treason.' He was practicing his Christian faith. God willing, he maintains his faith today."

I stepped closer to her and brought her close to my chest, hugging her tightly. Together we wept, with mixed relief at this news and sadness for what we had not been able to share until this moment. After a long embrace, she bent down before the candle, lifting it to light each of the other five candles, one by one. As she did this, I could hear her praying, "O God, forgive me."

She bowed her head in prayer. I placed my hands on her shoulders. In my mind, I could hear the bells pealing forth from the empty belfry above us. I was sure that Alexander, the dead, and Peter, the living, could hear them, too.

Too Many Voices

Troy, New York, 2007

Friday had come quickly. I had wanted to back out and put this off until another day, or another month. But I wanted to show Michael, my job counselor, that I could give it a try.

I had dressed up in my only suit, a white shirt, and a necktie. My dad had given me the suit two years earlier. I think I had worn it maybe four times. I had gone to Mass with him two times at Christmas and on two Easter Sundays. That was rough, with all those crowds of people around. I'd rather go there during the week, when almost no one is there. Just me and God. Maybe a couple of people saying their prayers. Also, on those days I can wear my regular jeans and T-shirt and sneakers.

But this Friday I had wanted to make the best impression I could. So I dressed up. Except for my shoes. They were too tight, so I preferred my old, ratty sneakers. I just hope people didn't look down at my feet.

Slowly, stealthily, I had crept toward the door of Rose's Florist Shop on Burdett Avenue. During the last two days, I had walked by, casing the place. It looked really nice. I sure hoped that I could get the job.

I thought about Michael's confidence in me. I had told him, "I'll do this for you." But he countered, "Why don't you do it for yourself, Jeff?"

So, with that thought, "This is for me," I counted slowly to sixty, breathing in and out slowly. Then I counted slowly to sixty one more time. Then I was ready, as ready as I ever would be.

I stepped into the shop. The "HELP WANTED" sign was still in the window. Good. I was glad there were no customers in the front. In fact, no one was around. On that June afternoon, the room was filled with the bright blossoms of orchids, lilies, and wildflowers. There were fancy bouquets in the cooler in baskets and jars of water. There were some silk flower arrangements on display on the counter.

Many of the flowers I didn't know by name, but they were beautiful. That reminded me of the American Beauty. Sounds like the name of a poem title, doesn't it? And the room smelled so sweet—almost too sweet—with the profusion of fragrances from so many different varieties. It felt like I was in the middle of my grandmother's outdoor garden.

"Hi there," a cheery voice exclaimed. At first, I didn't see anyone. But then, from behind the potted evergreens, peeked a smiling face. As she stepped out into full view, I saw a lovely woman, perhaps in her thirties, with short brown hair tucked into a floppy brimmed hat. She was dressed in a green sweatshirt and tan chino trousers.

"Uh. Hi there, yourself," I responded.

"May I help you?"

I looked down at my feet. Quickly, to redirect her attention away from my sneakers, I pointed to the sign. "I see you're still looking for help. Can I help you?"

I noticed that she was wearing old sneakers that looked older and rattier than mine. I felt relieved. In fact, I felt a bit overdressed. "I sent you a job application. I'm here for the interview with you. My name is Jeffrey Dempsey."

"Oh, yes, I have been expecting you. It's good to meet you. My name is Rose Bush."

"You've got to be kidding! Rose Bush?"

"No. No fooling. I used to hate my name as a kid. But it eventually grew on me. No pun intended."

I thought about my dad having told me that my parents wanted to name me Jack, after the prizefighter Jack Dempsey. I'm glad I am Jeffrey. I would probably have had to settle lots of fights with my fists if I had been named Jack.

I asked, "What do parents think when they choose names like that?"

"Well, mine wanted something sweet and lovely."

"Is that why you became a florist?"

"Partly, but I always have enjoyed working with plants and being outdoors. My name helps, too."

"Well, Mrs. Bush ..." I hesitated.

"You can call me Miss Bush. What is it?"

"Can I get the job?"

"Not so fast. Let's talk first," she said with a smile. "I was impressed by your resume. Especially by some of your references. I think what I need matches with what you want to do. Michael has referred some other people to me before. I trust his judgment."

"I don't know if you would want someone like me around here."

I really didn't know if she would hire someone like me. I recalled that the last job I had was mowing lawns in my neighborhood all summer after my junior year of high school. But then that fall I had quit the job at Hannaford's packing groceries after only working three weeks because I had argued with the boss. Not a smart move, arguing with the boss.

I had put in my resume that I had dropped out of school that October. I wrote that I had been in the hospital for two years and not worked for four years. She knew from my application that I lived in a group home with some other young men, and more recently in my own apartment.

Up until that fall, I had enjoyed school, gotten pretty good grades, and liked being around lots of friends. But then my symptoms began. I avoided drugs and alcohol but, still, everything started to fall apart. I started to hear voices that no one else heard. I saw things that no one else saw. Things got scary and different.

It was a rough time. I stopped hanging out with my friends at Troy High School. I stopped going out to parties on the weekends. I just wanted to stay at home, alone, in my room. I didn't want to be with people. I was afraid of everything, and everyone.

I remembered what had happened next. In January of my senior year, I had gotten angry and out of control. I threw a chair and a lamp at my mother at home. Dad had called the police, and the ambulance came. They strapped me down and took me right to Samaritan Hospital for emergency admission.

I had scared the shit out of my mother that day. It was months before she even came to see me in the locked ward. I still hate my father for calling the police and having me put away. For two long years, I was stuck in there.

It was hell. I was drugged most of the time. Everybody there was really sick. It was terrible. Over the past two years, since my release, I had been able to learn how to take more responsibility for myself. I hadn't had a crisis during the past six months. I had come to accept that I am a person with a mental disorder: paranoid schizophrenia.

For a long time I could not even admit that. As I was thinking, I realized Miss Bush was speaking to me.

"I do understand that you have an illness. But I understand that you have done a lot to learn how to control your symptoms. The important thing with me is that you can do the work here and like it. There should be no problem."

"Thank you. You sound so encouraging. I will try to do my best."

She continued: "I have an uncle who has trouble working because he suffers from depression. But he works in a sheltered workshop assembling parts of machinery."

"I know that I could not do assembly work. There is too much pressure. Besides, I don't like working with a lot of people around me." After a pause, I said: "I really would like working with flowers and growing plants. I used to work in the hospital garden, growing tomatoes and corn. I have a few plants in my apartment, and they're still alive. I am intelligent, too."

She replied, "Yes, I believe that."

"Once, while I was outside on the hospital grounds, a passerby stopped to change a flat tire. He didn't know what to do, so I instructed him, step by step, how to take off the bad tire, then put on the new tire. He told me he was amazed that a mental patient would know how to teach something like that to him. I told him, 'I may be crazy, but I'm not stupid.'"

I thought about how I had not even gone to my interviews for other jobs in the past couple of months. Of course, that is why they never hired me.

"Miss Bush, my mother doesn't think I should be working. She says that I should just collect Social Security for my disability. She doesn't want me to find out I cannot work like other people. She still treats me like a child. For God's sake, I am twenty-two."

She answered: "I can understand that. My mother doesn't think that I am mature enough to manage this floral shop. I received a degree in business management, and I've been working as a florist for ten years. Some parents can't let their children grow up and make it on their own."

I reached into my shirt pocket and lifted out a pack of Merits. She immediately lifted her hand, saying: "Sorry, but you can't smoke in here. You can smoke either in the back or outside."

"Well, I can wait a bit. That will be tough to work without smoking." I put the pack back into my pocket.

"You can have some breaks to smoke. But many of our customers don't like smoking in the shop area. It is hard enough getting people in to buy flowers with this economy. I don't want to give them any more reasons for going to another florist."

I replied: "I can handle that. Besides, it's not good for the plants either. I'll follow any of your rules. When can I start? I really need this job."

"Oh, I know. Don't worry."

"Worry? That's my middle name. Worry. Fear. Terror."

"Well, Jeffrey, when can you start working?"

"You mean I've got the job?"

"Certainly! You passed the interview. When do you want to start?"

"How about, ah, next Tuesday?"

"That's fine. Welcome to your new job. It's a pleasure having you on board." She extended her hand, and we shook hands.

"Thanks." I turned around to leave. "See you Tuesday."

She said: "See you on Tuesday, at one o'clock. Have a good weekend."

"Good weekend? I'll have a great weekend! I've got a job."

I stepped outside the shop. I paused to light a cigarette. I grinned and walked quickly down the sidewalk, starting to whistle.

I didn't even look down at my sneakers.

No Blue Cheese, Please

Troy, New York, 2007

We were standing outside the restaurant on Hoosick Street. Michael and Rose were talking before we went inside for lunch.

He was having a smoke.

"I wish you would quit," she said.

I shrugged my shoulders and smiled politely. I decided to keep quiet because I was a smoker, too.

Although Michael and Rose shared many thoughts and likes, smoking was their main area of disagreement. They had begun dating soon after I had started my job at her florist shop. This was the only subject that I'd heard them differ about.

Rose told Michael, "I'm worried about your health."

He replied: "I am, too. But it is a hard habit to break. When I'm ready, I'll stop."

As we entered the restaurant, the hostess greeted us. "Welcome to Friendly's. How many?"

"Three, please," said Michael.

The three of us had recently become good friends. Michael was my counselor, and I had gotten to know him better, he told me to call him "Mike."

As we sat down in the booth, Mike nodded to a young man wearing a Budweiser T-shirt and a group of his friends. Rose smiled and waved at someone she recognized. "That's David, one of my neighbors, and a good customer."

I asked her, "Is that why they call this Friendly's?"

"Could be," she answered. "They probably wouldn't attract too many people if it was called 'Enemy's.'"

Just then I noticed Timothy mopping the floor at the back of the restaurant. He had been working here for a few weeks. He lived with his friend Arnold in a small apartment on Eighth Street, across from my place. I had introduced Mike and Rose to Tim at Rose's florist shop, where I worked.

Tim saw me, and immediately his face brightened with a big smile. He waved and called out in a loud voice: "Hi, Jeff! Hi, Mike! Hi, Rose!"

Mike put a finger to his lips to signal him to be a little quieter. I beckoned Tim to come over and talk with us.

He placed the mop against the wall in the bucket and almost bounded over. He was an enthusiastic thirty-two-year-old. His blond hair was neatly combed back from his forehead, revealing clear blue eyes. His uniform shirt hung loosely over his pants. His brown work boots were wet from the mopping.

"What are you all doing here?"

"We came to watch you work, Tim," I answered.

"You're kidding me!"

"You're right. We really came to eat."

Tim inquired, "What are you going to have?"

I said: "I think I'm going to have a chicken salad wrap, with French fries. And a cup of hot coffee. It's cold out."

"Uh-huh! I like chicken, too." Tim looked at Rose, waiting for her answer.

"Me?" She paused to think. "I'm in the mood for a large tossed salad. With blue cheese dressing. And coffee, too."

Tim grimaced and scrunched up his nose. "I like tossed salad. But I don't like blue cheese. Yuck. I like yellow cheese and orange cheese."

Rose asked, "Have you ever had blue cheese?"

"No. I just don't like food that is blue. Besides, it smells funny."

"Well, maybe someday you can try it. You might like it. I enjoy trying new kinds of food. And I'm still alive to tell the tale."

Although no one had asked, Mike said, "I'm going to have a burger and fries."

I realized then that Tim and Arnold had tried many new experiences in recent months, just like I had. For all of their lives, they had lived in a group home with four other men who had developmental disabilities. When they moved into Troy and their own apartment, it was for the first time in their lives.

I said, "Tim, I remember when you moved across the street from me on August sixth."

"How do you remember the exact date?"

"Well, it was also the anniversary of the bombing of Hiroshima in 1945. The day you moved in I had been watching a memorial observance in Albany on TV."

Rose interjected: "Speaking of remembering, I just recalled that Mike and I had not answered your invitation to join you and Arnold for Thanksgiving dinner. We'd be happy to come to your home and be your guests."

"Oh, good! Great! I am happy you can come," said Tim.

Turning to me, he said, "You can come too, Jeff!"

"I'll be happy to join you. Thanks."

Tim replied: "Great! I'd better get back to my work, or my boss won't be happy with me. He tells me I shouldn't socialize so much with the customers. Here comes Jane, your waitress."

I told Tim, "Maybe someday you'll be able to be a cook or a waiter here."

"Uh-huh! Bye! See you later."

Rose replied, "See you later." Mike said, "Take care." I just waved goodbye.

One week earlier, on the first day of November, Arnold had come to Rose's florist shop. It was a clear, crisp day with a pastel blue sky and a few cirrus clouds high in the sky. All the leaves had fallen after a beautiful fall season.

Arnold was six feet tall, twenty-eight years old, with dark brown hair and thick moustache. He was wearing a bright red jersey and blue jeans. He shook Rose's hand and then mine but only smiled and nodded. He was somewhat shy, compared to Tim. He was developmentally disabled, like Tim, but he was also mute. He communicated with people using American Sign Language.

Arnold gave Rose an envelope with two names printed neatly: "To Mike and Rose." I came up behind her and watched over her shoulder.

As she opened the envelope, she announced with a flourish, "And the winner is ..."

Arnold hopped up and down, clapped his hands, and grinned.

In clear block letters, the note announced:

WE INVITE YOU TO OUR HOME FOR THANKSGIVING DINNER. ROAST TURKEY, MASHED POTATOES, STUFFING, CRANBERRY SAUCE, PUMPKIN PIE, AND COFFEE.
TIM AND ARNOLD

Rose told Arnold: "Thank you for your kind invitation. Mike and I will talk it over. We will let you know if we can come in a few days."

Rose had told me earlier that she and Mike had agreed not to answer any invitations until they had discussed the offer in private with each other. There had been a few times when each had responded affirmatively on behalf of both of them, ending with a conflict of two events at the same time and date. It was much easier for them to take the time to consider any invitation and to reply after they had talked together. I thought this was a good plan. Many times I had watched my parents argue because they wanted to do different things and couldn't agree which to do together. They could have used such a plan.

Arnold understood. He nodded his head briskly up and down. He gave us the OK sign, shook our hands, and turned to walk back home. I watched him as he approached the curb.

He paused carefully and looked both right and left. Then he quickly ran across Burdett Avenue.

I felt proud of him. I told Rose: "I remember how a staff person spent several days helping Arnold learn how to cross the street safely. It was one of the many new skills that Arnold and Tim had to learn at their new apartment."

A few days later, Rose told me that she and Mike had made their decision. "Mike's parents and sister live in Wisconsin. My parents are in Florida for the winter. Most of our friends are probably going to be with their own families for the holiday. We had not made any other plans. So we agreed that it would be wonderful to have dinner with Tim and Arnold."

Soon after our meeting at Friendly's, as Thanksgiving approached, Rose had asked what time dinner would be served. Tim replied: "In the afternoon. Maybe about one o'clock. It will take all morning to cook."

Rose asked: "May we bring something? I'd be happy to make a tossed salad."

Tim replied, "OK, but no blue cheese, please!"

"We will see," she answered.

One evening, Rose and Mike came to visit me at my home. Sometimes they would visit to discuss how my work was going, but this time they came for a social visit. I had made my bed and washed all my dishes and pans. I had even pulled up the window shades.

After they had complimented me on my housekeeping skills, we began talking about Tim and Arnold. I said: "Both of them are so polite and friendly. They are certainly different from what I expected when they first moved in."

"Right, Jeff," Rose said. "But they have not changed so much. Our attitudes and understanding of them is what has changed the most. But we had to be willing to give them a chance at first."

I shook my head and looked up at the ceiling, biting my lip. "Remember how some of my neighbors started a petition against any citizens like them living on the street? Although I had refused to sign the petition, I wondered if they would be a detriment to the community. I was afraid people would think I was like them."

Rose then said: "Once we got to know them personally, as individuals, we learned that they were not harmful or dangerous. They are probably better neighbors than some people who have lived here for years."

Rose turned to Mike and said: "It sure helped that you read a lot. When some of the people predicted that residents with developmental disabilities would lower the property values of the neighborhood, you were able to present the facts from other communities that contradicted that myth. Actually, you showed that property values often increased in such situations. It is hard to argue against facts from other places."

I responded: "I liked what one of the human service workers told the crowd at one of those meetings. He said they are people first and they have some special needs. They have rights like everyone else in America. Just like me."

Mike reflected: "It helps me to realize that neither of these men chose to be born with a developmental disability, just as with most illnesses. You didn't choose to develop your illness, Jeff. Yet people are often afraid of what they don't understand."

Rose moved over onto the couch next to Mike. He put his arm around her shoulder and brought her close. He gave her a big hug. They held each other closely for a long time. I began to think maybe I should go do the dishes or something.

Rose looked over at me and said: "Being friendly with Tim and Arnold, and with you Jeff, is like a big hug. We receive love from you. And you give love back to us."

Mike admitted: "I was embarrassed to realize that I thought I was open-minded about many issues. But I had some stereotypes about people with developmental disabilities. Each one is unique and individual. Each person deserves to be known as a person, just like you and me."

I interjected, "Yeah, just like you and me."

Rose smiled and declared: "We all make mistakes. Each of us has learned from Tim and Arnold. All we had to do was to allow ourselves the opportunities to get to know them better."

Mike concluded: "I am glad that we are all going to spend Thanksgiving with them. We can let them know that we believe that they are good neighbors. And our friends."

Rose added: "It is really sad that many of the other neighbors have not been willing to be open. Maybe, with time, they will come around to appreciate Tim and Arnold, too."

Mike stood up. "Well, Jeff, it's time for us to go home. Each of us has a busy day of work tomorrow. Good night."

"Good night," Tim said. "And thanks for coming over."

The next morning I saw the blue van come to pick up Arnold to take him to his job at the factory in Watervliet, where he assembled parts. Tim left later in the morning. I walked out of my apartment and up the street toward Rose's shop, feeling very warm and content. In my head, I heard the tune from "Mr. Rogers' Neighborhood."

Thanksgiving morning dawned cloudy and cold. But, for once, I was not bothered by the weather. I had many reasons to be grateful this year: my home, my job, my friends, my neighbors, my parents, and my health.

Even though I was not going to be eating at home, I spent the morning cleaning the kitchen floor. And I did the laundry down in the basement.

All the clean clothes smelled so fresh. It had been a long time since I remembered smelling everything so well. I had stopped smoking a week earlier. Although I still had a cough, I felt much more energetic. And I could taste and smell so much more.

I still heard a voice urging me to smoke, but I tried not to listen to it. When I saw a cigarette ad, I turned away.

At one o'clock, I went across the street to Tim and Arnold's. Arnold greeted me warmly at the door. He directed me to take off my coat, which he hung in the closet. I sat down in the living room.

As usual, their living room was bright and attractive. It contained a bright yellow-and-white-striped couch, three soft chairs, and a coffee table on a pastel blue carpet. Several houseplants, including some beautiful hanging ivy, were on the window sill in front of the large picture window. They had purchased all of their plants from Rose's.

Above the stereo set and TV were three large photo montages of Tim and Arnold and some of their activities. One showed different members of Arnold's family: his parents, grandparents, brother, and three sisters. Clearly, he had a caring and supportive family.

The second frame contained photos of Tim. His family members had all died. Most of the recent pictures were of different staff members or friends with Tim at parties and trips.

The third montage showed Tim and Arnold at various places in the past few years: a ValleyCats baseball game, standing by some cattle at the Schaghticoke Fair, camping and swimming at Cherry Plain State Park. They were holding some trout in one picture. In another, they posed with their team holding up their medals from the Special Olympics.

There was no doubt that they had led a busy and full life. Their home reflected their interests and their pride.

The doorbell rang. Arnold welcomed Mike and Rose inside. After Arnold hung their coats in the closet, Rose placed a large salad bowl and extra dishes in the kitchen.

Arnold tapped me on the shoulder after all of us had exchanged greetings and pointed to an ashtray on the bookcase. I told him: "Thank you, but I don't need that anymore. I stopped smoking."

He smiled broadly, shook my hand, and signed a gesture. At that moment, Tim came into the room and interpreted: "I am happy. I stopped smoking myself three years ago. It is something to celebrate."

Rose agreed: "Yes. I think all of us can be proud of that accomplishment, Keep it up. Maybe you can be a positive role model for your job counselor, too." She winked at Mike.

"Dinner is ready," Tim said. "Martha has been helping us cook today. So nothing got burned."

Martha was their residential counselor who spent a few hours each day with them helping teach daily living skills. She called out from the kitchen:

"Hi there! Happy Thanksgiving! All I'm doing is watching the clock. The men are doing everything else."

"Uh-huh," Tim grunted. "We can't read the clock very well. Martha tells me when to put what in, and when to take it out. Someday, we'll be able to do this all by ourselves."

Arnold rubbed his stomach, and I said, "That means his stomach says that it is time to eat."

In a few minutes, Tim came back out. "Arnold, can you help put the bowls on the table?"

We stood waiting expectantly while the food was placed on the table. Tim was wearing a large apron that read, "I am the CHEF."

Martha whispered in his ear, "You can take the apron off now."

"Uh-huh," he replied, taking it off, folding it, and placing it on the kitchen counter.

Arnold pointed to where each of us was to sit. Arnold signed the grace, which Tim interpreted: "Thank you, God, for this food and for friends. Amen."

I declared, "This dinner looks really good—almost too good to eat."

Rose responded quickly: "Well, you can sit and watch the food. But I am ready to eat it."

Tim carved the turkey at the table. Arnold passed the plates to serve the stuffing and red cranberry sauce. There were pickles, olives, and a large bowl of mashed potatoes.

Rose said: "You've made a wonderful dinner. What I like the most is that I didn't have to cook at all today."

Martha replied: "Good! And thanks for bringing the salad. Today, the gentlemen did most of the work."

Arnold gestured. Tim said, "He's telling you that he cut and mashed the potatoes."

He paused to think, and added: "And I stuffed the turkey. Martha was a big help."

She stated: "It was really a team effort. You two did most of the cooking. You can be very proud of yourselves."

Arnold nodded in agreement. Tim, his face flushing red, said: "Uh-huh. We are proud."

As I passed another small dish to Tim, he asked, "What's this?"

I said: "That is Italian dressing on the right. And blue cheese dressing on the left."

Rose added, "You have two choices, Tim." He wrinkled his nose, hesitated, and groaned, "Uh-huh!"

She emphasized: "You don't have to eat it. But I thought you might want to try it—even just a little bit."

He gingerly scooped a little amount of the blue cheese onto his spoon and placed it on the side of his dinner plate. He put some on his lettuce and tomato. He tasted some. First, he made a face, then added: "Not bad! Not bad at all. Better than I expected. Maybe I'll even have some more ... later."

We all laughed. Rose added: "I am glad that you are willing to try something new. That's all I ask. Thank you."

He smiled and replied. "Having you, Mike, and Jeff here for Thanksgiving is also something new, and special."

Arnold gestured. Tim said, "He wants to play cards."

I turned to Arnold and said, "After dinner is all over, we can play all the cards you want."

Rose asked Tim, "How did you learn to sign?"

"I went to school. I can speak. Arnold can hear. We make a good team, right? I wanted to be able to communicate better, so I studied in a class when we lived in the group home."

Rose replied: "That is really true. You make a good team. You are like brothers."

Arnold made a sign. Tim said, "He agrees that we are like brothers."

Rose asked: "Tim, could you teach me to sign some day? Then I could understand Arnold better, too."

"Uh-huh," Tim nodded briskly.

The conversation continued as we all enjoyed the rest of the dinner. We talked about so many different things. I was so busy talking I that didn't even hear any voices in my head. I felt really good. There were enough voices around the table.

Our plates were almost empty when Tim asked Rose, "Would you please pass the blue cheese?"

"Sure. With pleasure," she replied. "Do you want some more salad with it, too?"

"Uh-huh!"

Arnold gestured again.

Tim repeated, "He said, 'Save some room for the pumpkin pie.'"

My Sister, the Nurse

Humacao, Puerto Rico, 2007

On a warm, sunny morning, Manuel Loma walked up the hill with his mother and father. They were going to the grounds of the Ryder Memorial Hospital nursing school in the town of Humacao, located on the eastern coastline of Puerto Rico.

The dark brown eyes of the little nine-year-old sparkled as he spoke to his father. "I remember when Maria told me that she wanted to be a nurse."

"When was that?"

"It was the night she heard a woman from the hospital talk about the hospital at the youth club meeting. When Maria came home, she told me that she wanted to help people who were sick."

Senor Loma replied: "That's true, Manuel. Maria made clear her plans that night. But your sister began to think about being a nurse even earlier, while she was still in high school."

"Really?"

"Do you remember when I had my accident?" his father asked.

"Yes, Papa, I remember. You had to stay at the hospital for many, many weeks."

Manuel's father nodded. "After the accident at the sugar cane factory, my life was saved because of the emergency treatment and physical therapy here at the hospital. I think it was during that time when Maria began to plan on becoming a nurse. All of the members of my family were coming to visit me each day after school. Maria learned all about the people and the work that nurses and doctors do. And today she finishes out her year at the nursing school and becomes an LPN."

"I forget, Papa. What does LPN mean?" Manuel asked.

"It means licensed practical nurse, my son."

Manuel noticed that many other families had gathered and were finding their seats for the outdoor graduation. The Loma family found three folding chairs under the cool shade of some mango trees.

Senora Loma sat down. She added her reflections to the conversation. "Why, I recall something even further back than either of you have mentioned. Your grandmother lived here for the last two years of her life, Manuel. God rest her soul."

"Yes, of course," declared her husband. "She was seventy-five years old when we brought her here after her stroke. You probably don't remember her, Manuel."

Manuel tried to call her face to his mind but could only picture her photograph, which was kept in the living room. He looked at his mother's beautiful, thick black hair. Pointing to his mother, he said, "She looked like you."

His mother said: "Maria came to visit your grandmother often. They were very close friends and shared many stories together. I think that Maria began thinking about becoming a nurse then, when she was in the sixth and seventh grades."

Their conversation was interrupted as the band began playing some special marching music. The majestic processional had begun. The faculty members and speakers walked through the aisle, between the rows of families and guests, and up to the platform. Everyone was standing up, trying to see the graduating students, who followed and then sat in the front rows.

Manuel had to stand on his chair to see them. He exclaimed: "I see her! I see Maria! Isn't she pretty?"

Then everyone sat down again. The clergyman said prayers. Several special guests spoke. One of the speakers spoke in both Spanish and English and talked about the motto of Ryder Memorial Hospital: *"Lealtad; a Dios por medio de servicio a la humanidad."* That is, "Loyalty to God through service to humanity."

The speaker told them that the hospital had been founded as a Christian mission hospital. It had now become one of the best hospitals in the region, serving the needs of many people throughout Puerto Rico.

Manuel's eyes kept returning to Maria. She was seated in the front row of students. His mother leaned across him and asked his father, "When does Maria speak?"

Senor Loma said, "I don't know." They waited impatiently through the next speech. Then, finally, it was Maria's turn. The school's director introduced her, saying "The members of the class of 2007 have elected Maria Loma to be speaker for their class."

Manuel looked up at his parents, one on each side of him. Their faces were gleaming with pride.

"What will she say?" Manuel asked them.

"We don't know," Senor Loma said. "She wanted to surprise us."

"Be quiet," Senora Loma hushed them, placing her finger against her lips.

Maria rolled her motorized wheelchair onto the platform and waited until the director lowered the microphone to her level. After the audience stopped clapping, Maria began to speak clearly and firmly. She talked about the joys of sharing with her classmates and friends during their years of studies. She talked about parting to serve in different villages and cities around the island, continuing to learn after graduation.

She recalled some of the experiences shared by the students in her class. After each interruption of applause, she waited to continue.

She resumed her talk, saying: "Each one of you has entered the field of nursing for different reasons. Each graduate today can tell you about the education and background that brought him or her to this special day. I can only speak for myself."

Senor and Senora Loma and young Manuel listened intently to her remarks.

Manuel thought that she might tell them about the church youth meeting when she heard the lecture by the guest speaker who was a nurse. His father thought about his stay in the hospital after his accident at work. His mother thought about the care and visits to Maria's grandmother after her stroke.

"My friends, I began my preparation as a nurse to pay back a debt. Not a debt of money, but one of gratitude and love. Nineteen years ago, I was born here in Ryder Memorial Hospital. From the day of my birth, I have not been able to use my legs. But the doctors and nurses here helped keep me alive. They have taught my family and me ever since as I was growing up. Most of all, they taught me not to look at what my limitations are but to look at what I can do with what I have."

Manuel looked up at his father and gently whispered: "So that's why she wanted to be a nurse. We were all wrong."

Senor Loma leaned down to his son and replied: "No, we were all correct. Each experience of her life added to the others."

Maria continued and concluded her speech: "Through the help of many people over these years of my life, and the help of the love and care of God, I am now able to begin to pay back my debt to all those whom I love."

Manuel looked quietly up at his mother. He could see some glistening teardrops of joy and happiness slipping down her cheeks. Her lips silently formed the words, "Thank God."

Manuel smiled too and then joined everyone in their applause.

The Old Man

Humacao, Puerto Rico, 2009

"We must get going. Hurry up, Jose and Miguel!" called Papa Lopez as he loaded the blue Ford pickup with its last load. "Everything is ready to go! Blankets, charcoal, barbecue forks, basket, and all the food we need. All we need now is the family. Where is Pablo?"

Mama replied: "Pablo went to work in the lot next to Senor Fuentes' *casita* early this morning. He told me that he was not going to the beach with us."

Papa Lopez declared: "That's ridiculous. No school today. It's a holiday. I am taking a day off. We are *all* going. Sarita, go get him. Tell Pablo that we are all ready to leave."

A few minutes later, Pablo's sister returned and told her father: "Pablo insists that he is not going with us. He said that he has too much work to do in the vacant lot. He will eat lunch with Senor Fuentes."

Papa shrugged his shoulders and then nodded his head toward the truck. "All right. Let's get moving. Everybody in."

Mama Lopez and Sarita climbed in the front, with Pepe the dog. Jose and Miguel, the two older brothers, sat in the back amid the picnic supplies. Then Papa hopped into his seat and started the truck down the road. As they passed their friends and neighbors, they waved and hollered greetings.

One woman was buying fruit from the wagon that came out to the village three times a week. Some youths were washing a car with water from the stream beside the road. Little children were running alongside the edge of the tall grass. It was a beautiful, clear day for a trip to the beach, one of Puerto Rico's finest. Soon, the truck was out of the village, heading toward the highway.

This had been a busy day for Pablo. For several weeks, he had been gathering wooden beams and planks from different sections of his neighborhood. The best source was an abandoned sugar cane refinery. No one else had use for the lumber there. Some of Pablo's classmates in the eleventh grade had helped him carry the lumber. But none of them could find out what he was going to build.

Pablo had raked the refuse that covered the vacant lot next to Senor Fuentes' little house. He had piled it all into one corner. He had cut down the tall grass and undergrowth with his father's sharp machete. While his friends were playing ball or sitting at the store, Pablo had been busy clearing the ground of this useless plot of land. He had nailed the boards into large, flat sections that looked like three rafts ready to put into the water. Those platforms had then been been piled into another corner of the plot.

Each day Senor Fuentes had watched Pablo working after school. From his bed, he could look out the screenless window directly into the lot next door. It had been over a year since Senor Fuentes had suffered his second stroke. He was not able to use his left arm or leg. His partial paralysis, plus his severe arthritis, kept him confined to his bed. But he often told his sister: "I am blessed by God. I can still see clearly. I can still talk. I can still think, even though I can't leave this bed."

Senor Fuentes was called by most of the villagers *El Viejo*. He was known as "the old one" because he was over ninety. No one else in the village could remember further into the past than he could. He loved to tell stories about his days working in the sugar cane fields. He had retired from work long before the new oil refinery was built.

All of his family, his children, and his grandchildren lived in New York— all except his younger sister, Maria Garcia, whose husband had died when she was seventy-five. For the past two years, she had lived in the small four-room wooden house and taken care of her brother.

Both *El Viejo* and Maria belonged to the *Iglesia Evangelica Unida* in the nearby city. Their health and age prevented them from attending any of the services or activities. Once a month, the pastor came to visit them in the village. The church owned the empty lot on which the members planned to build a chapel in the distant future. Senor Fuentes once told his pastor: "I hope to see the chapel built next door before I die. I will live on the hope."

There was no church or chapel in Rio Abajo. All the families, whether Catholic or Protestant, had to drive or walk the six miles into the city. Many people would be happy when the new chapel was built.

Each day the old man watched Pablo working in the lot. He did not know what the young boy was planning. Very few people came to see Senor Fuentes, but every day, faithfully, Pablo stopped on his way home from school and came into the old man's room for a visit. They would talk about what had happened at school, about the baseball league heroes, about the activities in the village.

One day, Pablo began working early in the morning. He was busy sawing posts and hammering nails into them. He had borrowed his father's hammer, saw, and plane. His father was a carpenter but, on this day, while the family was at the beach, Pablo could use the tools all day.

Senor Fuentes could hear Pablo singing while he worked under the hot mid-morning sun:

"Gloria a ti, Jesus Divino!
Gloria a ti, pot tus bondades!
Gloria eterna a tus piedades!
Querido Salvador!
Gloria, gloria, aleluya!
Gloria, gloria, aleluya!
Gloria, gloria, aleluya!
A nuestro Salvador!"

It was one of Pablo's favorite hymns. He continued to work steadily throughout the morning, rarely stopping to rest. He set up corner posts and added braces, marking off the frame of a small building located in the center of the clearing. It looked like a toolshed, or maybe a playhouse. On the side facing Senor Fuentes's *casita*, Pablo left an opening for a doorway.

At noon, Maria Garcia called to Pablo. She stepped through the chicken-wire fence that separated the two yards. She said to him: "You work almost as hard as your father. You know how wonderful is his reputation as a craftsman and builder in this whole area."

"*Si. Muchas gracias,*" Pablo replied.

She continued, "*Por favor*, Pablo, tell me what you are making."

Pablo looked over at her through the black hair that had slipped over his forehead. His brown eyes sparkled as he smiled. "I cannot tell you, senora. Not yet. Maybe by nighttime, I hope."

"Well, I cannot bribe you. But you can come into the house now for some lunch with Senor Fuentes. It is all ready for you."

"Ah, *gracias,* senora. I am coming. I am starved."

He climbed nimbly through the hole in the fence and entered the little house. He felt immediately cool and refreshed. With a reminder from Senora Garcia, Pablo washed his hands in the kitchen sink. Then he went into the old man's room. It took a moment for his eyes to adjust to the darkened room. Pablo walked over and took his friend's hand.

"Buenas dias, senor."

"Buenas dias, mi amigo."

Pablo sat down in the straight-back yellow chair next to the bed. Senor Fuentes was propped up with two pillows behind his head. Next to the steel hospital bed there was a table with a radio, box of tissues, glass of water, and some magazines.

Usually Pablo would let Senor Fuentes speak first. But today Pablo was filled with some news. He had not been in to visit that morning.

He said: "Last night we had a very good Bible study and worship service with the men and boys in the city. We talked about the Psalms. I told everyone about your favorite psalm. Remember how you often ask me to recite it: 'I will lift up mine eyes unto the hills, from whence cometh my help'"?

The man nodded gently, squeezed Pablo's hand with a firm grasp, and turned to look out the window at the foot of his bed. Senor Fuentes said: "Whatever you are building out there, I hope it will not be two stories high. If so, I won't be able to see the high mountains in the distance. My special hills."

Pablo looked in the same direction. He could see the bare frame of his new building. The green, lush hills raised themselves above its shape. Senor Fuentes asked: "What are you building? You have kept it such a secret."

The young carpenter replied: "You will soon see. It is almost finished. I am building it so that you can see all of it when it is finished. And it won't block your view."

"That is good, my friend. All that I can see from here is this empty lot and the hills beyond. Someday our church will be building a new chapel there. But, in the meantime, the area might as well be used for play."

"Si, senor. It will probably be many years before our church can afford to buy the supplies and build the chapel. Our pastor said it would take a miracle to build it within the next four years."

"Es la vida. All good things take time," the wise man answered.

At that moment, Senora Garcia brought in a tray and set it on the bedside table. It included two glasses of orange juice, a flat dish containing about ten slices of fried banana, some toast, and a jar of guava jelly. Pablo and Senor Fuentes bowed their heads and closed their eyes, while Pablo gave thanks for the meal. Pablo then lifted the glass of juice up to Senor Fuentes' mouth.

He sipped through the straw and enjoyed the taste. The young boy nibbled on his favorite snack of a banana slice. The toast and jelly was for the man. Senora Garcia asked, "What have you two been visiting about?"

"Oh, nothing at all," her brother answered.

She smiled and said: "I think that you two have a secret. Pablo won't tell me what he is building out there. You say that you are not talking about anything. You are both like two little boys with your secrets." She turned about, laughing, and returned to her work in the kitchen.

Pablo and Senor Fuentes winked at each other. Pablo gave him a slice of toast, spread with delicious guava jelly. Senor Fuentes could hold the toast up to his teeth and enjoy the crunching sound. Pablo, in many little ways, was aware of what Senor Fuentes could do and what he could not do.

The old man finished his lunch and then asked, "Are you still planning to become a nurse and work in the city hospital?"

"*Si, senor*! In another two years I can begin training there. I must work hard in school so that I will be able to enter the training program."

The old man replied: "That is wonderful. We need good nurses and doctors. Those people at the hospital helped me learn to regain my strength. Maria can give me therapy here at home. I am fortunate to have such good care."

For quite a while, they talked about the hospital. Then the old man paused and changed the subject.

"You know, Pablo, God is still speaking. I had a good dream last night with a message from God. I dreamt that I would live to see the new chapel built next door. Every night as I watch the sun set over the hills beyond, I look forward to my dreams."

The young boy exclaimed: "Remember, you told me that old men dream dreams, and young men have visions? Well, you have taught me that God speaks still both in dreams and in visions. You should be able to dream some this afternoon during your nap. Now I must go back outside."

Pablo stood up, leaned over, and kissed his friend on his stubbled cheek. They shook hands and smiled quietly to each other. Pablo carried the tray back to the kitchen, visited briefly with Senora Garcia, and then went outside.

Throughout the afternoon, Senor Fuentes could not sleep. He kept busy watching Pablo's activity. Working under the hot sun, Pablo mounted the large flat panels against the frame. Because he had made them days earlier, he found it fairly easy to stand them up and attach them to the corner posts and crossbeams.

Later, he dragged a large sheet of corrugated steel and pushed it, by exerting all his strength, onto the top of the structure. He climbed up the side and nailed the hot roof to the beams. With the roof and walls completed, the inside of the building was dark.

The afternoon passed quickly. A short shower broke the heavy weight of the heat. Two of Pablo's friends stopped to visit with him. He sent them off, and they soon returned with some large paintbrushes and two large cans of paint.

After some discussion, they decided to stay and help Pablo paint the interior walls with white paint. Although he enjoyed working alone, he seemed pleased to have some help. When the walls were all white, Senor Fuentes could see their movements inside, through the open front doorway. With the job completed, the classmates waved goodbye. They went off down the road.

Pablo then stepped out in front of the new building, placed his hands on his hips, and looked admiringly at his project. He scratched his head and then disappeared out of sight for a little while. He soon returned from the corner of the lot with a board on which he had printed some large letters.

Senor Fuentes lifted himself up onto his right elbow to read the words. Only after Pablo had nailed the board above the front door and stepped down to the side could the man read the words: *"Dios es Amor."*

Those same words, "God is love," were also emblazoned above the pulpit in their church in the city. Now, for the first time, Senor Fuentes realized the purpose of the building.

Again, Pablo disappeared from Senor Fuentes' sight to the pile of lumber. He dragged back two long planks, which he nailed together, creating a large wooden cross. He pulled it inside the little building and placed it at the opposite end of the entrance.

By this hour, the shadows had begun to lengthen. The sun was settling down behind the hills, visible from the window. The color of the sky changed from blue and white to gray and pink as the clouds reflected the setting sun. Although Senor Fuentes could see the hills and the sunset over the roof of the new chapel, Pablo could not see them.

The young boy knelt down inside the building, in front of the cross. Senor Fuentes could see the young carpenter at prayer, his shadow outlined against the white walls. He could even hear a voice singing from within:

"Gloria, gloria, aleluya!

A nuestro Salvador!"

One hour later, Pablo was still in the chapel.

Senora Garcia called him: "Pablo, come quickly! I need you."

Pablo rushed out into the yard, climbed through the fence, and ran into the kitchen. He slowed down as Senora Garcia placed her finger to her lips. She pushed back the curtain hanging in front of the doorway that opened into the man's room. Senor Fuentes was peacefully lying on the bed, his eyes closed, a little smile on his face.

She put her arm around the boy's shoulder and softly said: "Pablo. He is gone. I just came in. He went without a sound, without a cry. So peacefully in his sleep, he died."

As a tear began to fall down Pablo's cheek, they both walked slowly over to the bedside. Pablo gently lifted Senor Fuentes' hand, which was already cool.

Pablo whispered softly: "It is finished. God is still speaking. Sweet dreams, my good friend."

First Night

Springfield, Massachusetts, 2010

I had been shopping for groceries with my four-year-old son, Miguel, trying to keep him from pushing the cart too fast. I knew that we could manage another week with my welfare check and food stamps. But there would not be much left over for Christmas gifts.

Soon, I thought, I would get a good job and be able to support myself. As I was thinking about what kind of work I could do, I had accidentally steered the cart into a young man about my age.

He was handsome, with a thin, black moustache, brown eyes, and curly dark hair.

"Excuse me. I need to watch where I'm going," the man apologized.

"No, it's really my fault. I wasn't paying attention," I replied.

My son interrupted, looking up between the two of us. "Hi! I am Miguel."

"Well, hello yourself. My name is Jose," he said as he bent down to shake hands with my son.

"I am Mommy's big helper. We don't have a daddy."

I winced at his direct honesty. Jose straightened back up, turned to me, and extended his hand. His handshake was firm but gentle.

"I'm Tina."

"Are you new in this neighborhood? I've never seen either of you before," Jose stated.

"We've just moved to this part of the city. I have lived across town all my life. I graduated from Commerce High School last year. How about you?"

Jose answered: "I went to high school in San Juan. I moved up here to join my brothers three years ago."

I inquired, "Where do you work?"

"I'm an auto mechanic at Benny's in the North End."

We chatted for a few minutes. Then I realized that Miguel and the cart had moved around the corner into the next aisle. Although I had wanted to keep talking, I knew my son could wreak havoc in a few moments.

Jose asked, "Can I call you some time?"

"Sure. Let me give you my number." I had decided, as a precaution, not to give my last name or address.

"Call me when you get a chance," I said, appearing nonchalant. We separated as I moved quickly to locate Miguel. It took a few minutes before my heart slowed back to normal.

I called out to Miguel: "Put that back where you found it. There is too much sugar in that." We finished shopping and soon were back home in our apartment.

Although it was small and sparsely furnished, our apartment was home, I thought. *It was good that we had moved out a month earlier from my mother and sisters' house. It was important for me to become independent. They were still only a couple of miles away, but this was our new home.*

It was four days before Jose called. *Four long days.* I thought. *Was he not interested in me, or had he lost my phone number?*

"I'm sorry I didn't call earlier, but I've been very busy at work," he apologized.

"That's OK. I've been busy, too."

Then, out of the blue, he asked, "Tina, would you like to go to a New Year's Eve dance with me?"

I hesitated a moment, catching my breath. "But I hardly know you. And besides, that's a hard night to find a good babysitter." I had really wanted to say yes, but I didn't want to sound desperate.

Jose continued: "It is three whole weeks away. In the meantime, we can get to know each other. We won't be strangers."

"I will have to think about it."

While I was thinking, Jose interjected, "As for a babysitter, my younger sister is willing to look after your son on New Year's Eve."

"How do you know she doesn't have other plans?"

"Because I already asked her. Besides, she is at the age when she would rather earn money babysitting than going to a dance. Of course, that can change any time, as soon as she discovers boys."

"Well, yes, I'd be happy to go with you, as long as she can babysit. I don't have any other excuse."

Our conversation was interrupted because Miguel had wanted my total attention. Jose promised that he would call the next night.

When he called the following evening, I was in the middle of cooking supper. Jose suggested that we get together three nights later at a sandwich shop.

"You can bring Miguel with you. He has to eat anyway."

We agreed to meet Friday at 6 o'clock. I appreciated that Jose was willing to include my son on our first date, rather than exclude him. He seemed to care about both of us, as a mother-and-son team.

I looked forward eagerly to Friday evening. I wore my bright red winter coat and high black boots. Underneath, I wore a green woolen sweater and a long green skirt.

It was cold, with a bitter wind blowing, and there was the threat of snow from the dark clouds. Jose was dressed casually in a white shirt, blue slacks, and a black leather jacket. He wore a gold chain necklace and a large emerald ring.

When he greeted me at the restaurant, he peered behind me. "Where's Miguel?"

"I left him playing with the neighbor's children. I felt better coming alone, even though you invited him," I replied.

We ordered sandwiches and coffee. The place was crowded with people from the neighborhood. The food was inexpensive but home-cooked. After we talked a bit about the day's events, Jose became serious. He leaned across the table and said earnestly: "There is something I have to tell you before we go any further. I want to be completely honest with you."

He paused, and I thought to myself: *He's going to tell me that he is married with children. It will be over before we have even started.*

Jose continued: "I am a recovering alcoholic. The New Year's Eve dance is for sober alcoholics and addicts and their friends. It is sponsored by the church so that we can have a sober evening."

I was so relieved. No wife. No children. Recovering from alcoholism—I could handle that. I stammered: "That is no problem to me. The dance will be very nice. I don't drink anyway."

Jose looked relieved, too. "I was afraid that would be an obstacle to our being friends. I have been sober for almost two years. One day at a time. Last New Year's Eve I spent with some sober male friends. This year I am looking forward to spending the first night of the new year with a lady friend."

"Lady? It's been a long time since anyone called me a lady. I was fifteen when Miguel was born. I had to drop out of school for a year to care for him. I did not want to marry his father, so I chose to raise Miguel by myself. Most people don't call an unmarried teenage mother a lady."

Jose replied: "Well to me you are a lady. You have good manners and style. You are polite and caring. You have healthy values."

"Thank you for the compliment," I said. "And you are a gentleman, too. I am excited about going to the dance with you. I have gone to a few other dances in the past year. But every man has come on too strong and aggressive." There was some certain, and definitely sincere, characteristic about Jose that allowed me to trust him. Most men had not been worthy of my trust.

"Tina, I am not usually so forward with a woman. But I do feel comfortable with you. I believe you are a real lady."

After that first supper date, Jose called me every night after work. He asked me: "When is the best time to call you? I know that you are busy with Miguel, and I don't want to interrupt your time with him."

I told Jose: "Most nights after nine is the best time to talk. Then, he is generally asleep, and I can relax."

So each night, shortly after nine, Jose called me. I had made certain that Miguel had had his story time and bath and was tucked under the covers early enough so that he would be asleep by the time Jose called.

One time, when Miguel was still awake, Jose asked to talk with him. Once Miguel knew Jose was on the phone and had briefly talked to him, he went right to bed.

I had become accustomed to men flirting and teasing me in public. I did not like it, but I had gotten used to that type of treatment. Jose was different. He always treated me with respect and dignity. That meant a lot to me.

Whenever we talked on the phone, we talked about what had happened during the day. He told amusing stories about the people he worked with at the garage. He told me about the adventures of replacing a water pump or a carburetor in a way that kept me enthralled. But he also took his work seriously and took pride in his ability as a top mechanic.

In turn, I told Jose about the trials and tribulations of being a single mother. There were many antics and anecdotes to share about Miguel's activities. Although Jose did not have any children, he was interested in my son as if he were his own. It was a pleasure to have someone who was interested in Miguel and in me.

We talked for hours about our past, our present, and our future dreams. He told me: "Every other girl I have dated also drank a lot. Our activities revolved around parties, drugs, and booze. Now I am ready for someone who can be fun and sober at the same time."

Jose told me about his three other jobs that had ended because of his drinking. He had been discharged from the Army because of incidents involving alcohol. He told me: "I have messed up a lot of my life. But the past two years I have kept this job. I have gained back my self-respect. I don't want to go back again, but I don't want to forget my past. Those memories help me stay sober one day at a time."

Jose was definitely a different experience for me. So many of the men I had known in the past had boasted about their drinking exploits and their crazy adventures. Jose was able to talk about his past honestly and to share his plans and goals for the future.

One night I told Jose: "New Year's will be a special first night of the year for me. I hope to get a job and get off welfare. I want to begin a new life for Miguel and myself. I have had an interview to be a bilingual receptionist. In early January, I could be hearing from them."

Jose radiated confidence and assurance. He said, "I know that you will do well in any job that you accept."

I realized that I was ready to become serious about this man. But I also planned one day at a time. I had been looking for a person who would care about both my son and me. So often in the past few years, a man had been interested in Miguel but not in me, or in me but not in my son. Jose was clearly a man who showed true interest in both of us as individuals with our own specific, personal needs.

During Christmas week, I visited Jose during his lunch breaks. I went to a Christmas party with his fellow workers at a lounge near the garage. The other men were pleasant, but Jose was definitely special. When I talked with some of his friends, he did not appear jealous or protective. He trusted me and was secure.

First Night, or New Year's Eve, finally arrived. Jose's sister had met Miguel the week before. They had no trouble settling down to play together when Jose and I left the apartment.

As we left, Jose said to Miguel, "See you next year, little guy."

Jose was dressed in a formal suit with a fancy pink shirt, shiny black shoes, and a long, gray winter coat. He looked very handsome.

I had altered my junior prom gown, made with yellow silk, by adding a large white bow on the back.

"Wow. You look great, Tina!"

"Thanks. So do you! I feel great!"

We drove to the church in his '96 Ford. The parking lot was filled with cars. It was a clear, bright night with the stars sparkling above. It was cold as we rushed into the building.

The auditorium was dark, with bright lights coming from the corner where the DJ was already playing the latest CDs. Many green and white balloons and crepe paper streamers were hanging from the ceiling and walls. Tables and chairs were set up along two sides of the dance floor.

I did not recognize anyone except Pedro and Sarita, a couple I had known from high school. Jose knew several people, and he introduced me during the course of the evening. I felt comfortable and accepted among many of his friends.

There was one table filled with a group of noisy men, but they did not bother me. We sat with three other couples, including Pedro and Sarita. Jose and I danced together for five fast songs in a row, completely enjoying the fast movement and excitement.

After a while, we sat down to rest. For the next half hour, I talked with Sarita and Jose about Miguel, and we exchanged stories about our children's lives. Pedro and Sarita had two sons, ages three and five.

Jose offered to get me a soda. While he went to get some drinks, Sarita turned to me and said: "Maybe we two mothers have been talking too much about our children. We can trust that they are having fun at home, or that they are all asleep. When the men return, let's try to avoid talking any more about the kids for tonight."

"Maybe you're right. I forget how much of my life is wrapped around Miguel. I need to put some focus on myself and have fun tonight."

Jose returned with the soda, and we all talked for a while. The next dance was a slow one. Jose asked, "Would you care to dance, my lady?" He bowed graciously.

I smiled, stood up, and curtsied. "My pleasure, sir."

As we returned to the dance floor, I put my arms around his shoulders. I was determined not to talk about Miguel. I could see Sarita dancing a few yards away from us. I winked at her, and she winked back at me.

An hour later, we were still on the floor, dancing both fast and slow numbers. I was going to get the full amount of pleasure out of this evening.

I asked him, "Are you making any resolutions for this new year?"

"Actually, Tina, I made so many promises that I didn't keep in my drinking days that I want to keep it simple this year. My only resolutions are not to pick up a drink today, to go to meetings with my friends to help me stay sober, and to take responsibility for my life."

I replied: "That may be simple, but it is very important. I know that you will do your best to keep those resolutions."

"And how about you?"

"How about me, what?"

"What are your resolutions for this year?" Jose asked.

"Mine are simple, too. I resolve to be a good mother, taking care of Miguel, and be good to myself. I resolve to get a good job so I will not be dependent on welfare."

"Well, Tina, I know you can keep those resolutions. And I promise to help you."

Jose continued: "This is one New Year's that I will remember with joy. There were so many in the past that I don't remember at all. I had to ask my friends what I said and did the next morning. I like having a clear head and my own memory back."

As we kept on dancing, I felt really wonderful being held so close. We moved about the floor slowly and gracefully. I felt as if we had been dancing together for longer than one evening. Much of the time, we were silent, enjoying the moments together.

The rest of the evening I managed not to mention Miguel, although I did think about him every once in a while.

Just before midnight, Jose said: "I have a suggestion. Since we have spent this evening together, just the two of us, maybe we could plan something tomorrow for the three of us."

My eyes brightened. I was touched by his thoughtfulness.

"That's a great idea. After we wake up, we can go sledding in the park. There is still enough snow on the ground. Miguel would love that."

Even though I had stopped talking about Miguel, here is a man who was still thinking about him, I thought. *He cares about both of us.*

Shortly, too soon it seemed, it was midnight. It had seemed so right to be dancing in Jose's arms, holding him closely.

At the stroke of midnight, I gave him a hug, saying, "Happy New Year!" I reached up and gave him a light kiss on his lips.

He replied, "Happy New Year, Lady Tina!" This time, the kiss lasted much longer. It was a wonderful First Night.

And it was the beginning of a truly new year filled with promise for all of us.

The Washington Park Snowman Contest

Troy, New York, 2011

On a cold Monday in January, I called Billy as soon as I had finished breakfast.

"Did you hear there's no school today? Look outside; there's got to be over two feet of new, good-packing snow!"

"How do you know it's good packing?"

"I just went out to check it. It is perfect."

"Are you ready to have our contest today?"

Billy Santorini and I lived in the Park Place Apartments on Third Street in Troy.

I had lived there eight years—since I was three—with my parents and my grandmother. While they were at work, my grandmother looked after me most of the day.

Billy had moved into our building last September. We were in the same grade at school.

He lived with his mother. They both went to Mass at St. Joseph's Church several blocks away. Billy was glad to know that our building had once been the parochial school for St. Mary's parish.

He told me: "When I am home, I sometimes feel like I am still in school. It helps me focus on my homework."

His father had come back from duty in Afghanistan seriously wounded. His parents ended up divorced a few years after his father's return.

We weren't exactly friends. Sometimes we played well together. Other times we'd fight something awful. I was bigger and taller and often picked on him because he was short and thin.

My ground-floor apartment faced onto Washington Park. Billy's was at the back on the second floor.

That winter had seen a record snowfall, and the snow was piled up on the sidewalks along all four sides of the park. Inside the park, all the benches and small trees were completely covered. Only the large, bare trees stood above the snowy ground. But many of the storms had been light and dry, not very good for packing.

During the last snowstorm in December, we had both made snowmen in the park.

Billy declared, "Mine is better than yours."

I said, "No way."

"Uh-huh!"

That day, we had argued for twenty or more minutes.

Finally, he ended our battle, saying: "Let's agree. After the next good snowstorm we can have another contest."

"But next time we will have rules to keep from arguing."

My grandmother helped us make the rules. That had been a good idea. She had taught me lots of rules and manners from the old country, Ukraine. She had moved to America after the fall of the Soviet Union, when life was very difficult there. My parents came over when they were young.

"I'm just as ready as you are, Richard Malenikov," he answered. He sounded defiant. "We can start as soon as I get my coat and boots on."

"Let's double-check our rules," I said cautiously. "I have them written right here." I read them to Billy over the phone: "Each contestant can use only snow from within the park. Only natural objects can be used for decorations. No one else can help in building or giving ideas. The snowman must be completed in three hours or less. There will be three judges, acceptable to both contestants. The decision of the judges will be final."

Billy replied: "Sounds all right to me. Maybe we'd better make sure that our judges will be around when we finish."

"We don't need to check. My grandmother will be home all day looking after me. She can watch us from our window."

Billy said, "Officer Thompson will be coming by in his cruiser around noontime."

I said: "Our third judge, your mother, will be on her postal carrier route. She will be coming by to deliver mail at our building just before noon."

Billy and I met outside at nine and started to make our snowmen. We used the open area of Washington Park. We had already planned for this day by getting permission from the park association to have our contest there. The park is privately owned by the neighbors, who pay to take care of the park. It is surrounded by a black wrought iron fence on all sides with two locked doors. The snow was so high that we could climb right onto the piles and then over the fence opposite our building.

The big, sticky snowflakes had stopped coming down. We were dressed with heavy coats and hats. We had plenty of natural material. But it was also very cold.

Billy said, "I'm glad that I have new, black, waterproof mittens."

"You can say that again."

He repeated, "I'm glad that I have new ..."

"OK, OK, I get it."

We kept an eye on each other all the time. The first hour, each of us gathered snow from all around to make two large piles before we started to make the shapes.

A neighbor stopped to talk with Billy. I listened very carefully and said: "Hey, don't get any ideas or help from anyone else. That's the rule." The neighbor waved to me, smiled, and moved on.

I made a huge St. Nicholas sitting on a big chair, like a throne. It was like the chair in which the bishop sits in the cathedral. My snowman was bigger than life-size. I remembered icons of our patron saint inside our family church, St. Nicholas Ukrainian Orthodox Church.

Most of the leaves from the trees were completely covered up by the snow. We could not dig out many of the branches or leaves. Because the natural snow was the only element we could use, we had to depend on our skills at shaping and molding our glistening, bright figures.

"Hey, Billy! Remember when your mother donated the big living room chair to Troy Area United Ministries? My snowman's chair looks like that one."

He answered: "I really loved passing on what we no longer needed. When we moved here, my mother bought some new furniture. Their furniture program is a big help for others who can't afford furniture, like beds, dressers, and tables."

"I wonder if we can help as volunteers there. Maybe we can help load or unload the truck. We should check that out."

"I think we have to be a lot older and can drive the truck. We have to think of some other way to help."

While I was working on St. Nicholas, Billy was building a standing figure of the superhero Iron Man. He was standing tall, with his hands on his hips. Iron Man was all white but with smooth, metallic-looking armor. He was as large as my snowman but much more threatening and powerful.

I asked, "Why is this your favorite superhero?"

He replied: "Because he does good to protect the world from evil. I like how Richard Stark invented the suit of armor and fights for good. If my father had been wearing the same armor, he would never have been wounded. He would have come back healthy and would not have left us."

"But your father is still a real hero for fighting in Afghanistan."

"Yeah, my dad is a human hero, and Iron Man is a superhero. I need both of them."

Most of the time, we worked hard without talking. We focused on making the best snowmen we could.

"My Iron Man will not last very long."

I asked, "Why not?"

"When he blasts off with his boot rockets, it will melt the snow all around."

Finally, Billy yelled over to me. "Time's up! It is three hours!" With our work done, we each stood back and admired our large statues. Now, we could relax.

We crossed the street and found Officer Thompson. He came to Grandma's apartment. A few minutes later, we stopped Billy's mother when she came to our front entrance with the mail. We entered my family's apartment.

"Boys, take off your boots and coats."

We hung our clothing on the rack inside the door. It was good to be inside.

"I'm freezing. I can hardly feel my hands and feet," Billy said.

Mrs. Santorini and Officer Thompson did not need to be prompted. They placed their coats on the coat rack and took their boots off.

Billy's mother looked around the large room and smiled. This was the first time she had been inside.

Sonya Malenikov's apartment was filled with sunlight. It had high, white ceilings and bright red and yellow paintings and fabrics on the walls. There were many Ukrainian objects around the living room.

Mrs. Santorini said, "This is such a beautiful apartment."

Grandma said: "When I moved here from Ukraine I could not bring much. I found furniture and drapes from local shops and tag sales. I bought much of this from the antique stores in Troy. One of my favorite shops is Olga's Shop, on Second Street. She is wonderful with her help with fashion and interior design."

"Well, you have done a wonderful job making this into your new home," Mrs. Santorini said.

"It has been a hard winter," Grandma said. "Much like the winters where we lived in Odessa on the Black Sea. It is good to have a warm place to live."

The three judges looked out from my grandmother's window over at our new bright, white creatures, the saint and the superhero. Billy and I stood anxiously at the far end of the room while they whispered and discussed our work.

My heart banged like a drum. Billy tried to act as if he didn't care who was going to win.

Finally, Officer Thompson turned to us and said, "We remind you that one of your contest rules is that the decision of the judges will be final."

Billy and I both nodded in agreement. He said, "Uh-huh."

I barely heard my grandmother explain: "Boys, this was a difficult decision. We believe that Richard's snowman was a better figure, a very impressive saint. But Billy made a really powerful-looking Iron Man. That is why, overall, we chose Billy's as the best of the two."

My throat tightened. I felt hurt and bitter toward Billy. He was watching with a smirk on his face. For once, I didn't want to look back at him. I felt like I wanted to beat him up.

Billy declared: "Thank you. I accept first prize."

Officer Thompson said: "But we have decided to give first prize for the best in two categories: one first prize for the sitting snowman and another first prize for the standing snowman. And since you are the only two contestants, each of you wins first prize. Congratulations."

Billy said, "I will accept this new change with one condition."

I turned in surprise toward him. "Hey, we both won. What is your problem?"

He smiled and put his hand on my shoulder. "Richard, first we have to accept the decision of the judges. I suggest that we form a partnership."

"Partnership? You mean work together?"

"Today, we've been rewarded for the best snowmen on our block, in our park. We could make an even better snowman working as partners. Rather than compete against each other, we can be a team. OK?"

I put my hand out and shook Billy's hand. "OK, partner. I would rather work with you. It might even be more fun than fighting against you."

He said, "It sure won't hurt me as much as getting beat up by you."

I hugged my grandmother. Billy hugged his mother. And we both shook Officer Thompson's hand.

Grandma said: "I have made a special prize for both of you, and for your judges: a cup of hot Russian tea and a tea cake."

On the counter was a beautiful brass samovar, where the tea was brewing. Grandma had set out china tea cups and a plate filled with her homemade cakes, one of my favorite traditions from her old country. Besides, she always reminded me, tea is better for you than soda.

We all celebrated the contest and shared our prize.

Billy said, "Now we have to wait for the next good snowstorm."

I said: "They say two heads are better than one. Four hands must be better than two hands."

"We will try to be the best team competing with the others who join us," Billy said.

"Grandma, will you help us make up some better rules to include more people?"

"Rules, rules, I am good at making and teaching rules. One will be no fighting. You both can learn to cooperate and settle disagreements without violent words."

Billy said we can be a team helping people. "I went over to the dinners a few times at Troy Area United Ministries. Maybe we can help to serve food. That would be in the spirit of both St. Nicholas and Iron Man. Sure beats fighting against each other."

I suggested, "We can call ourselves Team Richard and Billy."

"No way. It should be Billy and Richard."

"How about the Washington Park Team?" I asked. "Then neither of us gets first credit."

"Yeah. That sounds good."
"OK, partner!"
We smiled and shook hands.

About the author

Robert Loesch, 71, was born in Florida and attended schools in Massachusetts, New Jersey, Ohio, and Connecticut. He has lived and worked in New England and upstate New York. Most of his career has been in parish ministry and human services. He has traveled extensively, including to Puerto Rico and Russia. Since 2006, he has lived in Sand Lake, New York, where he serves as pastor of Zion's United Church of Christ.

Most of his published writing since 1966 has been in non-fiction. This is his first collection of short stories.